CHILL FACTOR

Also by Aaron Marc Stein

CHILL FACTOR

AARON MARC STEIN

PUBLISHED FOR THE CRIME CLUB BY

DOUBLEDAY & COMPANY, INC.

GARDEN CITY, NEW YORK

1978

All of the characters in this book are fictitious, and any resemblance to actual persons, living or dead, is purely coincidental.

Library of Congress Cataloging in Publication Data

Stein, Aaron Marc, 1906-
    Chill factor.

    I. Title.
PZ3.S819Ch [PS3569.T34]   813'.5'2

ISBN: 0-385-13556-4
Library of Congress Catalog Card Number 77-11754

Stein

*In
Memory
of
Berenice Safferson*

CHILL FACTOR

GUILT FACTOR

I

I like snow. No snow, no skiing and, I, Matthew Erridge, have had too many winters on one engineering job or another when I was tied down to one of those hot places where you never see even the first flake and where Christmas, like a Fourth of July that's slipped its moorings, must, for want of any of the things that make a proper Christmas, be celebrated with fireworks. Lacking Norway spruce, a man can make do with Roman candles, but nobody's ever dreamed up a satisfactory substitute for snow. Even the whitest sand won't do it.

I'd like to think that, if the weather predictions hadn't left it with a promise of snow and had indicated that it was going to be too much, I might have contented myself with tossing another log on the fire and watching through the windows the whitening of Mom's New Jersey garden, but I know myself better than that.

I would have headed north to the ski slopes anyhow. The way it was, though, despite the barometer boys saying heavy snow extreme cold, even the more cautious types just switched into the thermal underwear and a heavier sweater and went charging out into it.

I had snow tires. I had a good heater in the Porsche. I had a good supply of Virginia Gentleman along for inner warmth and I also had a big thermos jug of hot coffee. I was wearing the thermal long johns and a sweater that had been knitted in

Norway where they do their knitting with sub-Arctic weather in mind. On the car seat beside me I had a sheepskin coat. To my way of thinking I was starting out overequipped, but that came of Mom's having been around to superintend my departure. If Mom weren't the wrong sex for it, she'd wear both a belt and suspenders.

Heading out of New Jersey, a man doesn't have to go far to get himself a bit of skiing. A short run to the west takes him into the Poconos, a short run to the north gives him the Catskills, but Erridge had his sights set on bigger things: he wasn't going to content himself with sliding down any molehills—he was off to Vermont and real mountains.

I was out on the road. I had gassed up and I had a good hour's driving behind me before the first tentative flake came drifting down. Quickly the fall thickened and, by the time the second hour had passed, I'd had my fill of observing how pretty it was with every branch and twig grown fat and white and all the ground turned soft and downy and everything cleaner than a TV wash.

Also the fall was approaching the point where what was coming down blocked out all sight of what had already fallen. It was caking on the windshield and steadily the wipers were less and less successful in keeping ahead of it. It made little difference because, when I squinted through a segment left briefly clear in the wake of the wiper blade, I could see nothing before me but the falling flakes. They were blotting out everything. The air seemed to be solid with them.

It was zero visibility and I was driving north into country where this snow had had an earlier start. If there were any other cars on the road, I wouldn't be seeing them until they were within a foot or two of me. From time to time I would be aware of one as it passed going the other way. If there was anything ahead of me or behind me, I didn't see it. Nobody was putting on any speed under those weather conditions and nobody had any ideas of overtaking.

I told myself that there wouldn't be many cars out. Only the nuts would be driving and it was the middle of the week when most nuts would be at work. How many lunatic engineers could be between jobs at the same time and wandering at large in the same area? All the same I was holding Baby down to low speeds and I was keeping a sharp watch. Those passing southbound cars became fewer and fewer and then gradually I realized that there hadn't even been any of those for what was a very long time. I got to feeling that the whole world had gone away somewhere.

I had set out with the delusion that I was going to make time. At breakfast Mom had stoked me up good. Since I hadn't wanted to have to wait out some waitress in a lunch joint along the road, she'd packed me a great stack of hefty sandwiches and a sack of doughnuts. With those and the coffee, I could eat in the car.

I had been figuring on making it all the way before dark would set in, but I hadn't gone more than halfway when it became obvious that I would be forced to give up on that. It was going to be only another couple of miles before night would catch up with me. I began thinking motels, but thinking wasn't enough to bring any of them in sight. Maybe I was on a stretch of road where there was nothing and maybe what was out there was a strip that was solid with motor courts, but I had no way of knowing. There was nothing visible.

I shifted the gears of my thinking. Since there seemed not to be a hope that I could get off the road before night, I would just go on forging ahead while I waited for the dark. Then lighted windows at the side of the road would be show-

ing through the falling snow. The glare of neon would pene-
trate it—even if with no more than a glow reflected off the
falling flakes.

The dark closed in and I did see a glow, but it was only
what came from my own head lights. I pulled up and
switched off my lights. There was the possibility that their
glare reflected off the snow had me so much dazzled that I
wasn't seeing any other lights. I sat in the dark for a minute,
giving my eyes time to adjust, but I saw nothing and I
couldn't give it any more time. Even though I had the feeling
that there could be nobody else out on the road, sitting out
there without lights Baby was a menace to navigation.

I switched the lights back on and worked at getting Baby
rolling again. There was nothing for it but to keep going. For
a bit there, however, Baby's wheels just spun. I held my
breath till the tires bit in and we started creeping again.

It was a warning. I was going to have to count on seeing a
light while I was still in motion. I was not going to be able to
risk another stop if it was to be only for reconnoitering.

The next time I stopped it was from no choice of mine. I'd
come to a place where drifting snow had piled high on the
road, and that was it. I was stuck. There was no going forward
and I was reasonably certain that there couldn't be much going
back. The way the snow was drifting, it had to be that the
road I had just come would also be blocked.

If I was going to find a place to hole up till the snowplows
came through, it had to be up ahead. I wasn't out on the western plains or in Texas range country where the roads might
run for miles and miles without even so much as a shack
turning up at the roadside. I was in the overpopulated North-
east. Refuge couldn't be too far ahead.

It was there. It had to be, but I couldn't count on Baby to

bring me any nearer to it. What a car can do, Baby can do magnificently, but even she has her limits. I was snug enough in the car. I had one of the windows rolled down the necessary crack so that enough fresh air was coming in to ward off any chance of monoxide poisoning. The air that was coming in was increasingly wind-driven and increasingly cold. The thermometer was dropping to subzero levels, but I had the car heater going and I was warmly dressed and I still had most of the sandwiches and doughnuts and coffee. I could stay where I was with the motor running to keep the heater going and I would be in good enough shape unless I ran out of gas before the snowplows came through.

The big question was how soon a snowplow could come through. The odds had it that all up and down that road there would be other cars trapped in the snow, and each of them would be an obstacle to the snowplows. Clearing that road was going to be a slow process. I'd have to be crazy to expect anyone to get to me before the gas ran out and the cold would take over.

There had to be something up ahead. There might not be any motels, but there would be houses. My plans hadn't called for cross-country skiing, but a couple of miles of cross-country would be no hardship. There could even be some pleasure in them after the hours behind the wheel. I had muscles all over me that were screaming for a stretch. I could strap on the skis and push on ahead. If I didn't leave the engine running while I was away, I'd be conserving gas against the possibility that, finding nothing, I might be forced to return to Baby and hole up in her.

That was my first thought and I liked it, but almost immediately I had a second thought. If I was going to make the try at it on the skis, I had to count on being away from the car for at least a couple of hours—an hour for exploring up ahead and then another hour or more for working myself back in the event that I found nothing. The way the temperature was dropping, I could call it a certainty that after two hours Baby's engine would have gone too cold for any hope of getting the heater going.

I could forget about conserving gas. If I was going to take off on the skis, it would be an all-or-nothing effort unless I left the motor running while I was gone. I checked the gas. The needle showed three quarters of a tank, enough to last a long time.

I opened the car door. It took some hard pushing to force it open. Even though the door was at the side away from the wind, just in the time I'd been stuck there enough snow had piled up against it to hold it against even a heavy push. It was only by launching all my weight into it in heavy lunges that I forced it open. That was going to be another problem if it turned out that I'd have to come back to Baby: I would probably have to dig the door free. I decided to worry about that when the time came.

The wind blasting in through the open door felt colder than you'll ever believe. I didn't even want to guess at where the temperature stood. In that wind it felt as though the mercury had to be frozen in the thermometer. You know how the wind will do that. It's what the weathermen call the chill factor.

I hauled myself out of the car and dragged the sheepskin after me. I had a scarf and I wrapped it around my nose and ears and chin. I shrugged into the sheepskin coat, and yanked the hood up over my head and pulled the drawstring tight. I had some good, warm gloves, but they were going to have to wait till I had the skis down off the roof of the car and had clamped them on. I had to work fast. Fumbling at clasps and clamps with heavily gloved fingers would get me nowhere, but doing the same fumbling with fingers gone stiff and numb with the cold was going to be no better. I do carry a flashlight in the glove compartment but getting the skis off the car roof and on to my feet was a two-hand job. I didn't stop to bring the flash out. I was intent on getting the job done while the fingers were still good for something. Working at it in the dark was no help either. When you have nothing to go on but touch, the going can be rough. When the numbing of your fingers is turning touch off as well, the going gets a lot rougher.

I was so concentrated on my problems and wishing so hard that I could have some light that, when it came, my first reaction to it was simple gratitude. It helped. It was a moment or two, at least, before it occurred to me to think about where the light might be coming from. It made the falling snow a gleaming dazzle. It was a bright light. It had a lot of glare packed into it and it was set full on me. I stood there for a moment, just staring into it. I raised my arms and waved them. I shouted. In that moment, though, the light veered off me and disappeared and a louder roaring was added to the roaring of the wind.

It was a snowmobile and it was moving off. I gave out with a couple more shouts but, quickly realizing how futile that was, I shut it off. A guy on a snowmobile hears nothing over the noise his machine is making. I must have been so intent on getting the skis down off the car roof that I hadn't heard it coming toward me.

It wasn't a night when even the wildest of snowmobile nuts would be out roaring around just for the kicks. I had never thought that the things could be good for anything, but in these conditions they had it over anything on wheels. Certainly it made sense that the locals would be out on their snowmobiles to search the road for drivers marooned in the snow. That would be a rescue operation that could be mounted before any snowplow could break through. This, after all, was the snow belt—even though it had probably never been belted this hard before—and guys around here would be likely to own snowmobiles.

I had a moment of thinking it might be smart to leave the skis on the car roof and climb back into Baby to wait my turn for the snowmobile rescue, but I didn't like the thought much. Sitting around waiting to be rescued has never been Matt Erridge's style. I was itching to be on the move, and it wasn't as though I'd been thinking of going anywhere where the snowmobilers couldn't find me. I was just going to be moving on up the road. If my guess was good and they were patrolling the road, they'd pick me up just as easily out of Baby as in.

All the time I was thinking I was working at getting the skis down off the roof and clamping them on. It took time, but I did get it made before my hands were totally useless. I hauled on my gloves and banged my hands against my thighs to get the blood moving back into my fingers.

It was only when I started moving that it first hit me that I was going to have a problem staying on the road. Once I was out of range of my head lights, I was moving in the dark, and the way the snow had drifted, the road borders were obliterated. Moving over to the side, I came up against something that felt like a tree trunk. Moving to the other side, my hand touched another tree trunk.

I went back to the car, remembering the flashlight. I had to fight the door open again, but this time it was easier. Fresh snow had been drifting against it, but it hadn't been long enough for a heavy accumulation.

I brought out the light and switched it on. It didn't give me much, but it would have to do. As long as I kept to the edge of the road, the flashlight did pick up the tree trunks. It would only be when I ran out of trees that I would have a problem. I'd think about it when I came to it.

Moving along that way, totally concentrated on trying to pick up the next tree and watching for any glow that might indicate a lighted window, I had no eyes for anything that lay directly ahead of me. When I came upon the car, the first I knew of it was when I banged against its rear fender.

My first thought was that some idiot had it sitting across the road and without lights. Then I had the more generous thought that the battery might have run out. As I came edging around it, I realized that there was no telling whether its lights were on or off. Both the tail lights and the head lights were out of sight. The snow had drifted high above them.

I shone my flash into the car and I saw the man. He was an old man with a wrinkled face and arthritically swollen knuckles. His thin hair was gray except at the back of his head where blood had darkened it. He was slumped down over the steering wheel and he was absolutely still.

I wrenched the car door open and reached across to the driver's seat to touch him. I laid my gloved hand on his back. I could feel no movement, not even the slightest rise and fall of breathing. I hauled off my glove and touched his face and hands. He was cold. I worked my hand inside his coat and his shirt and felt for a heartbeat. There was none.

Bent into the car that way even for those few moments, I began feeling suffocated and dizzy. I pulled back out and filled my lungs with air, breathing until my head had cleared.

With the door hanging open, the car's dome light was on and I noticed that the windows were rolled up all the way. No safety crack had been left anywhere for bringing fresh air into the car and the exhaust pipe, buried in snow, was blocked. I reached back in to turn off the ignition, but there was no ignition key. It would have been too late in any case even if the motor had been running. The man was dead.

I reached past the body and tried to open the door beside the driver's seat, but, even though it was on the side away from the wind, the snow was drifted so solidly against it that I couldn't move it. I settled for rolling down all the windows and letting the wind blow through. When I pulled back out, my hands were wet. It was only then that I realized that the man's clothes were soaked and that the body was sitting in a pool of water that had gathered on the car seat.

It didn't seem possible that any one man could have sweated that much, least of all such a dried-out little old man. As soon as I thought about it, however, it was obvious that it wasn't sweat. I'd reached inside his coat and his shirt to feel for a heartbeat, and his shirt and his skin had been dry.

I couldn't worry about that. I had to think about what I could do about him and, since I had satisfied myself that he was past help, there was nothing for it but to leave him as he was. I had to fight down my feeling that there should have been something I could do, but that was just emotion screaming at me. It wasn't sense.

I rolled the windows back up and shut the car door. Until the storm died down and the road was opened up again, he was as good where he was as anywhere. I was telling myself that I had to go on, but I was having trouble making myself leave the body. Then I did something that made me feel a little better about it. Don't ask me why it made me feel better. I pulled the door open again and flipped the switch that would keep the dome light on even when the door was shut. I wasn't leaving him there in the dark.

Up to the time I had come on the car there had been an exhilaration in forging along through the snow and the wind and the cold. Now it was just hard slogging. I kept turning around and looking back even though there wasn't anything much to see, only the falling snowflakes brightened by the glow of the light in the old man's car.

It wasn't long before even that was gone and all I could see behind me was the endless curtain of falling snow. I pushed on, forcing myself to concentrate on watching the line of trees to keep myself on the road and on keeping my lookout for any lighted windows.

I heard it before the light started coming up behind me. It was the whining thunder that grew in the roar of the wind. I turned and waited. Soon the snowflakes were gleaming with light. There was a steady brightening and a steady increase in the sound. Then as though something had come down and slapped a lid on it, the sound stopped and there was only the noise of the wind. The light, however, held constant, although it didn't match the intensity of glare I'd seen when I'd been taking the skis down from the car roof.

It was a snowmobile again, but it had stopped. It was just standing. I worked toward it and now I could move fast—I could return along my own ski tracks. There hadn't yet been time for the falling and drifting snow to obliterate them. As I came closer, I could make a guess at the distance. The snowmobile had stopped about where I'd left the dead man in the car. Someone else had now found the body.

When I came up on it, it was some moments before I could see anything; I'd blinded myself with staring into the light.

Pushing past it, I came up against the snowmobile. I was seeing nothing then but floating green clouds. I shut my eyes in an effort to rid myself of them but they went on drifting across the inner surfaces of my eyelids.

A hand came down on my arm. It took hold and squeezed.

"You okay, mister?" a voice asked.

It was a gruff voice and unsteady.

I opened my eyes and tried to see. I made out a bulky figure that seemed to be the only stable thing in a shifting green emptiness.

"I'm okay," I said. "There's a dead man in that car."

"Yeah, and there's bound to be more of them. Stuck in this snow, trying to keep from freezing to death, holed up in the car with the motor running to keep the heater going and with all the windows shut to keep the wind and cold out, they're like committing suicide. The monoxide gets them."

"This guy hit his head," I said.

"Yeah. I saw. About you? You out of the empty Porsche down the road, the one with the ski rack on the roof?"

"Right."

"I've been looking for you, mister. Where did you think you were going?"

"I was looking for a house. A night like this people would take a man in."

"Sure. But how the hell were you going to find any house in this stuff?"

"Sooner or later I'd see a lighted window," I said.

My vision was clearing. I could see the man now. He was a big guy, tall and wide and thick across the shoulders. In one of those padded jackets he looked enormous, but I could judge that there was a big hunk of man inside the padding. I could see his hands. They were a big man's hands with thick, solid wrists.

Like me, he had a scarf wrapped around most of his face and he had a woolen stocking cap pulled down over his ears. So there wasn't much to see but the big padded bulk of him and his hands and his eyes. By the way he carried himself, I guessed him to be a young guy, maybe somewhere in his twenties.

"You weren't going to see any lighted windows," he said. "Not tonight you weren't, because tonight there aren't any. The snow broke down the power lines and we're getting along on candles and firelight. The little of that showing through a window isn't enough to carry more than a couple of feet."

"Are there any houses nearby?" I asked.

"I'll take you to my place," he said. "We can't make you comfortable but tonight nobody else could either. It's dry and there's a fire. I was about to pull him out and take him back with me, but he can wait. I'll take you first and come back for him."

"No," I said. "Take him. Just tell me how to get there. I can make it on the skis."

"Not in a million years, you won't," he said. "I know it blind, but there's no way I can tell you, no landmarks you can see. You'll go right past it without knowing it's there."

I turned my flashlight down at the snow. His snowmobile track showed up clearly. I called it to his attention.

"No problem," I said. "I'll just follow your track."

He hesitated, but he seemed to be having the feeling I'd had and that I was now having again. Past all reason, there seemed to be something indecent about leaving the dead old man alone there in the storm.

"Okay," he said. "You keep to my track. I'll cart him home and come right back to pick you up."

"You don't have to do that," I protested. "I can make it all the way."

"No need for that. I'll come back for you, mister."

"Erridge," I said. "Matt Erridge."

"Sobieski," he said. "Stan Sobieski."

He stuck his hand out and we shook. He had a good strong grip but he didn't work at it.

I helped him get the old man's body out of the car and load it on the snowmobile.

"He was a nice old guy," he said. "It's terrible he should have to go like this."

"You knew him? He was a local?"

"Has a place near here. Came summers and weekends. Mr. Hoffman. He was a good old man. Everybody liked him. He was everybody's friend."

He started up his snowmobile and took off with the body. I started following along in his new-laid track, but then I had another idea. Food and energy crisis. He had just come from looking at my car. The snowmobile had laid a track I could follow back there. I'd turn off the engine. Also I'd left the whiskey back there and the sandwiches and doughnuts. The food wasn't much but, for people cut off from everything, even a little extra might help. I was certain my two quarts of Virginia Gentleman would be welcome while we were waiting for the road to open up.

I headed back to Baby. Moving along in the snowmobile track, I made time. I hadn't realized how slow my tree-to-tree progress had been. Back at the car I found the snow drifted against the door. I unclamped one of the skis and, using it as a shovel, I got enough snow cleared away so that I could jerk the door open. I stowed the whiskey bottles in the pockets of my sheepskin and, turning off the engine, I pocketed the ignition key. Carrying the sack of food, I headed back the way I'd come. This time I was putting on all the speed I could get up. I had to. New snow was drifting over the snowmobile track, and I had to make it back at least as far as the dead man's car before it was completely wiped out.

I hadn't gone more than part way before I again heard the snowmobile and saw its light. It had stopped, but this time the light was sweeping back and forth. Stan Sobieski was looking for me. I shouted, but I knew it wasn't carrying; I knew the wind was blowing my shouts away, and I reserved my breath for keeping myself on the move.

As I came closer, I could hear him shouting. The wind was in the right direction for carrying the sound to me. I no longer needed the flashlight to show me the track. I could just aim myself at the snowmobile light and plug on. I tried using my light as a signal, waving it back and forth as I hurried toward him. He caught it and, starting his snowmobile up, he came charging along to meet me.

"You went the wrong way," he growled. "I thought I'd lost you. I didn't want to lose you."

The words look better than they sounded. He was snarling them at me.

"Sorry," I said. "I didn't mean to worry you. I had something back in my car. I just went back to get it."

"A fool thing to do." He was still growling. "I could've run you back there if it was so important."

We piled onto the snowmobile and took off. That for the time wiped out any further talk. Have you ever ridden one of those things? I know what people mean when they talk about something blowing your mind. That noise does it.

He was right about the hopelessness of my search for lights. We were off the road and almost within touching distance of his house before I could make out the faint, flickering glow that showed through his windows.

He opened the door and hurried me inside. We were in a dark hall. He had shut out the wind and the snow, but the cold was in there with us.

He opened another door to a flickering of light.

"Come in here," he said. "This room's got the fire. It's the only place in the house that's even half warm."

Have you ever been in a house in the country where everything is electric-powered and the power lines are down? Your lights go, your oil furnace goes, your water pump goes, your cookstove goes. All of a sudden you're a Pilgrim Father with none of the skills and almost none of the equipment.

The room with the fire was all right. It had a big fireplace and there was a roaring fire in it. In the light of the fire and some candles a young woman with the help of a middle-aged couple was making up beds on the floor, mattresses laid on the floorboards with sheets and pillows and blankets.

"Sally," Sobieski said, "this is Matt Erridge. He's the one I was telling you about. You know, on the skis." He turned to me. "My wife, Sally, and Mrs. Kelly and Mr. Kelly. The Kellys are here out of the storm like you."

The young woman ignored him—the way they do when a guy's in the doghouse. She made an elaborate show of it. She turned to me.

"It's not going to be as comfortable as I would have liked, Mr. Erridge," she said, "but we're doing what we can."

"It's great, Mrs. Sobieski," I mumbled.

My mind was on her eye. She was a fine-looking, upstanding girl, but she had the most terrific shiner. It was more than a black eye. It covered almost half her face. I guess she saw me staring at it, because she quickly turned away. She finished what she was saying with only her undamaged profile turned toward me.

Her husband meanwhile was shrugging out of the padded jacket. He was even bigger and huskier than I'd thought and, with the scarf unwound from around his head, he was showing a fighter's face. There was the crooked line of a broken nose and some scarring around the mouth and chin. I was thinking he'd picked a bad night for hanging a mouse on the little woman.

II

I set my bag of sandwiches and doughnuts on a table and put the bottles down beside them.

"Some food and drink," I said, "for anybody who wants any."

Sobieski scowled.

"That what you went back for?" he asked. "We've got stuff."

His wife took a more gracious tone.

"Thank you very much," she said. "We're going to need it, the way some people are around here."

She was talking to me, but she was talking at her man. He caught it.

"I haven't just been standing around doing nothing," he said.

She ignored him.

He went to the fire and with great care he set another big log on it. He was a man who took pride in his fires. The log had to be placed just right. Alongside the fire there was a crib with a baby in it. Satisfied with his placement of the fresh log, Sobieski turned to the baby. Gently he touched the back of his hand to the baby's cheek.

"He's getting too hot," he said, shifting the crib a few inches.

He was obviously trying to make peace with his wife. She wasn't having any.

He picked the baby up out of the crib and sat it on the flat of his big left hand.

"This is Firpo," he said.

"The child's name is Stanley," Mrs. Sobieski said.

Again she was talking to me and at him.

"I call him Firpo," Sobieski said. "He was a fighter, an Argentine, Luis Angel Firpo. My grandpop used to talk about him. They called him the Wild Bull of the Pampas. This one's the Wild Bull of the Pampers. He's wet again."

His wife grabbed the baby away from him. He let it go but not without a protest.

"I can do it," he said. "I'll change him."

She said nothing, but the look she gave him was telling him to get lost.

For a moment or two he stood with his hands dangling, watching her change the diaper. The kid made some happy-baby noises and she responded with loving-mother noises. It was just herself and her baby. She was shutting him out. I saw his hands clench up and I saw the effort with which he unclenched. It seemed to me that the girl was asking for a mouse on her other eye.

He turned away from her and stood studying the fire. He scratched his head.

"Got to rig something to cook on," he said. "Like something to hang a pot on."

"Let me help," I said.

"If you have any ideas, Matt," he muttered. "I been trying to think. I don't know how to begin."

"You don't have a barbecue or a hibachi or anything like that?" I asked.

"Barbecue out back. We grown-ups'll be all right. But even if I dig out the barbecue and get a fire going, she can't stand out in the snow and the wind warming Firpo's bottle for him."

"If we can dig the grate out of the barbecue," I suggested, "we can rig something in here."

Grinning, he whacked me on the shoulder.

"You stay here and keep warm," he said. "I'll dig it out."

"With two of us, it'll go faster."

"If you want," he said.

"Have you got two shovels?" I asked.

"Only one snow shovel, but there's one I use for ditching."

"Okay," I said. "Where are they?"

Sally Sobieski, busy with her baby, was giving us no attention. The Kelly pair, however, were eying us with obvious hostility. There were two camps in that house. I could see that, prior to my arrival, Sobieski had been standing alone. Now it seemed to be that I had been assigned to his camp. The two of us were the enemy.

Sobieski led the way out of the house. It was only a few steps to the barn, but we were fighting the wind. It obviously had been a considerable time since anyone had used it for a barn. He had no farm animals in it, and even the old barn smells of hay and cattle had left it. He was using it as a garage. He had a car in there and a pickup truck. Otherwise it was garden tools and a workbench with a few hammers and wrenches and screwdrivers. If the guy was a do-it-yourselfer, it had to be in only the most modest way. There was nothing there you'd call a workshop.

Stretched out on the floor was the old man's body. Sobieski had covered it with a tarp, but the tarp wasn't long enough.

The dead man's feet were sticking out. When I turned my light on the tarp, Sobieski squirmed.

"I was going to put him in the house," he said. "The other rooms are so cold, nobody can go into them. I brought him in, but that Mrs. Kelly, she got the screaming hysterics. She couldn't be in the house with a dead man. Her nerves. She's the kind beats a man over the head all the time with her nerves. Before I even had them out of their car, I could see that. I had to move him out here."

"Don't let it bug you," I said. "He's past caring."

We picked up the shovels and, bucking the wind all the way, we battled our way around the house. It was his turf and he knew it well. Even though his barbecue was completely covered over with snow and not even a white hump to mark its location, he went straight to the spot and started digging. I set to work alongside him. We didn't have to dig it out completely, only down far enough to where we could get a grip on the iron grill and haul it out.

He picked it up and started toward the house. I headed back to his barn-garage. Quickly he came after me and grabbed me by the arm.

"The house is this way," he said.

"I know," I told him. "We need more than the grill. I saw something I think we can use. I'll go get it. I won't be a minute."

He came with me. Maybe he was still worked up about the time he'd thought he lost me out in the storm. He seemed unwilling to let me out of his sight. We worked our way back around the house. It was easier coming that way because now we had the wind at our backs. Out front we came on another big guy. He was standing out there on snowshoes and looking at my skis. I'd left them propped against the house wall along-side the door.

Sobieski introduced us.

"Matt Erridge—Bert Dawson."

Dawson put out his hand.

"Glad to see you," he said.

He was another one with a good, strong grip, but this guy worked at it, one of those babies who makes an act of aggression out of every handshake.

"Glad to be here," I said.

"There's this couple," Sobieski said. "They're inside. They're okay, but there's old man Hoffman."

"He out in this?"

"Go on inside," Sobieski said. "No good standing out here in the cold. We'll be right in. I'll tell you."

"Where you going?" There was an edge of wariness in the way Dawson asked.

"Just over to the barn for a minute. We'll be right back. Go on in."

"I'll go with you," Dawson said.

It seemed to me that they were like kids who, finding themselves in hostile territory, cling together. I got to think-ing about primeval impulses, of men confronted with savage nature and reaching out to each other, of the beginnings of community.

We headed toward the barn. Dawson on his showshoes did better than Sobieski and me. He was in the barn ahead of us. When we came in, he was just beginning to turn back the tarp that covered the old man's body.

"Gees," he mumbled. "How did it happen?"

"No telling exactly," Sobieski said. "He was in the car with the windows shut tight and he was gone. You could figure the monoxide got him, but he's got blood on his head."

Dawson hauled out a handkerchief and blew his nose hard. He tried to make it look as though he were dabbing the snow off his face, but he was doing his dabbing at his eyes.

"The gas must have been getting to him," he said from behind his handkerchief. "I guess he got out of the car and tried to make it on foot but he fell and hit his head. Then, he must have crawled back into the car and passed away there."

That "passed away" grated. This bird was talking like an undertaker. He was older than Sobieski, but he was just as big and almost as rugged. He looked as though he'd had ten more years and they'd put the first traces of flab on him.

"Poor old guy," Sobieski mumbled. "I hate leaving him out here."

He told Dawson about Mrs. Kelly and her nerves.

"Yeah," Dawson growled. "Women."

There was no profit in any of that. I went over to the thing I'd spotted when we'd been in there earlier. It was one of those big iron washbasins. There was rust on it and it looked as though it hadn't been used in years. Obviously Sally Sobieski would have a washer and dryer. She wasn't half old enough ever to have bent over a washboard and a tub. I picked the thing up.

"This'll do it," I said. "Let's get it rigged before it's time for Firpo's next bottle."

"Right," Sobieski said. "She's mad at me now. No use making it worse."

"I better get back to my place," Dawson muttered.

"Come in and have a drink first," Sobieski told him. "We're more than all right for booze. I had some in the house and Matt here brought some."

"I don't know. I left a fire going. I don't want to leave it for long. I could come back and find the house burned down. Tonight that'll be all I need."

"Just a quickie," Sobieski coaxed.

"Okay, a quickie," Dawson agreed.

Back in the house I went to work on the improvisation of an indoor barbecue. Social amenities of sorts were going on around me, but I was staying out of all that. I set a couple of big logs parallel on the floor near the fire and put the washbasin on top of them. I pulled out of the fire a couple of logs that were past the flaming stage and were just glowing a bright red. Dumping them into the tub, I rested the grill from the barbecue on top of the tub.

Nobody was paying me and my operation any attention. They were occupied among themselves. Dawson had set it off with his greeting to the woman of the house.

"Gees, Sally," he said. "Where did you get the eye?"

Sally countered question with question, but the look she tossed at her husband carried the answer.

"Where does any woman get an eye like this?" she asked.

"Yeah," Sobieski said. "That's me. Stinker Sobieski, the wifebeater."

"He thinks it's funny," Sally said.

"I don't think it's funny," Stan protested. "It's my fault. I'm not saying it isn't, but Christ knows I didn't mean for it to happen. I left a rake lying around outside. She went out and in the snow she didn't see it. She stepped on it and the handle came up and got her in the eye. It's my fault. I'm sorry. I been saying I'm sorry."

He sounded more sore than sorry and among explanations for a black eye, it was one of the classics. I wondered whether it was true. Sally was neither confirming nor denying.

He had poured out drinks all around, and when he tried to

hand her hers, she turned her back on him. He set it on the table and left it there. I picked it up and took it to her.

"Don't you like my whiskey, Sally?" I said.

She took the glass from me.

"Thank you, Matt," she said. She walked over to the grill and she gave me a beautiful smile. "And thank you for this," she added. "I don't know what my baby and I would have done."

They were all occupied with the whiskey, but there was something that was bothering me. I slipped out of the room. Stan came after me. He caught up with me out in that cold hall.

"The john's upstairs," he said.

"And your pump isn't working," I told him. "I'll go outside and see if I can still write my name in the snow."

"It's so cold out there, do you think you can find it?"

"I'll find it," I said. "I've had it a long time. I have a general idea of where to look."

He laughed and let me go. Just in the few minutes we'd been inside the wind had died down. The snow was coming down as heavily as ever but now the air was still. I could slog my way to the barn without too much effort. I had no wind to fight.

I'd taken my flashlight with me, and I worked as fast as I could. I didn't want anyone to wonder why I was taking so long and to come out to look for me. Even though I was hurrying, I made certain I was doing a thorough job. I went through the dead man's pockets, but not bothering with any of the things I was finding in them. I was looking for only one thing.

I went through all his pockets twice and I didn't find it. He had no keys on him. I started back toward the house, thinking as I went. After all, I hadn't searched the floor of his car for the keys. There were all sorts of possibilities. The way we took the body out of the car and loaded it on the snowmobile, his keys could have fallen out then and been lost in the snow.

Outside the barn I remembered my excuse for going out of the house. It seemed a good idea.

Heading back to the house, I remembered my skis. I'd left them leaning against the house wall, and it seemed better to stow them in the barn. Picking them up, I headed back. I had my flashlight in my pocket. I'd been back and forth between house and barn now so many times that I could do it in the dark, following the trail of my own footprints in the snow.

I had my hand on the barn-door latch when it hit me. A hard smash at the back of my head took me down, and I went out.

I came out of it cold and wet. My head was aching and there was a ringing in my ears. I tried to shake the ringing off, but I quickly gave up on that. Just moving my head even slowly broke the headache away from its moorings and started it swishing around sickeningly inside my skull. I tried to pull out of the snow and get my feet under me. That was worse. I gave up on it before I blacked out again. I was telling myself that I couldn't just lie there. The cold was cutting in on me. I was thinking that I should have been minding it and I wasn't.

I'd read stuff about how a man felt when he was freezing to death. As I remembered it, he sank into a pleasant drowsiness, dropping away to a comfortable and even luxurious finish. I had the drowsiness, but it wasn't pleasant. Maybe the headache was in the way and maybe that guy who wrote the description didn't know what he was talking about.

I promised myself that I'd give it only a minute or two and

then I'd make a try at moving. I kept that promise to myself or at least I think I did. Things weren't too clear. The way I remember it, I struggled to my knees and the snowflakes started going the wrong way. Instead of floating straight down in the windless air, they took to whirling around me. That headache inside my skull was going clockwise and so were the snowflakes, and it seems to me I knelt there in the cold trying to figure out whether it was my ache that was making the snow go around that way or vice versa. It seemed important at the time.

Thinking about it was doing me no good. With my numbing hands I reached out for the barn door. Door or wall, if I could lay my hands on it, I might be able to find a handhold that would help me pull myself to my feet.

I groped in every direction and I could find nothing and I'm not talking about a handhold. I couldn't even find the barn. It would have been then that I crumpled and blacked out all over again because that's the last of what I can remember, if it is remembering and this bit wasn't just a dream.

When I did finally come out of it, it was with a light in my eyes and hands pawing at me, and voices going back and forth above me.

"You take the light," one of the voices was saying. "I'll carry him."

I wanted to say I didn't have to be carried. I wanted to say I could walk. Stan Sobieski crouched down beside me and heaved me up over his shoulder in a fireman's carry. He wasn't bothering to be gentle about it and when he tried to rise up with my weight on him, he did some slipping in the snow. It was a rocky ride back into the house. It also seemed to me that he was carrying me a long way, much more than the distance I remembered between the house and the barn.

Somewhere en route I passed out again and the next time I came to, I was on the floor near the fire and I was surrounded. Mrs. Kelly was rubbing my wrists. Sally Sobieski was mopping at the back of my head. Kelly was trying to force whiskey between my lips and it was dribbling all over my chin. Stan was taking the boots off me. I pulled up on my elbows and for starters I worked at getting the whiskey inside me. I didn't need it pouring over me; I was wet enough without it.

By that time Sobieski had my boots and socks off and Kelly, leaving me to do my own drinking, moved down to my feet. While his wife was rubbing my wrists, he was rubbing my ankles. Stan took hold of my pants zipper. My belt had already been loosened and the waistband unhooked. I grabbed at his hand.

"Leave that," I said. "I'm okay this way."

"The hell you are. You're half frozen in those wet clothes. I'll give you a pair of my pants. They're only work pants, but they're dry."

"These'll dry in no time here by the fire," I argued.

He slapped my hand away and yanked down the zipper.

"Firpo's got more sense than you've got and he hasn't got any," he said. "Relax, man. They're married women. They've seen a guy in his underwear. They'll live through it."

I had to admit that he was making sense. Those thermal long johns were all the cover anyone could need and, even if they weren't, so what the hell? Nudity isn't what it used to be. Everybody goes to the movies.

Once he had my pants and shirt off, I could see the steam come up out of the long johns in the heat from the fire. The warmth felt good. It was a while before he came up with those work pants he had promised me and with a lumberjack shirt. He was just letting me lie there and steam till the long johns had dried on me.

"You've got a small cut on the back of your head and a big lump," Sally told me.

"I know," I said.

I knew a lot more than that but I wasn't about to go telling them. I was waiting for what they would tell me.

Stan did the telling.

"Matt," he said, "you've sure enough got a head on you. The way you fixed it so Sally can warm Firpo's bottles and even hot things up for the rest of us, that's great, but you're also a dope. So you had to go. So what? You do it right outside the door. The snow will cover it up quick enough. You don't have to go off into the woods and hide. Nobody was going to come out and watch."

"Is that what I did?" I asked.

"Off into the woods." he said. "With the snow covering everything up, you couldn't see tree roots or vines or whatever and something like that tripped you and you fell and hit your head."

I could have told him that when a man trips over something, he's going to topple forward. If he does hit his head in the fall, it's not going to be the back of his head. I was wondering if it was possible that he didn't know that. I said nothing. I let him go on talking.

I had gone out. Bert Dawson had finished his drink and had refused a second. He had to get back to his place and keep an eye on the fire he had going. Stan had seen him out of the house expecting he'd find me out front. When I wasn't anywhere in sight, he hadn't worried.

"But then I realized you had been gone a long time," he said. "I did get to worrying. I went out and looked around for you again. By then the wind had gone down and it was all still out there. I hollered for you, but you didn't answer. The others heard me and Kelly came out. It was then I noticed that your skis weren't where you'd left them."

His first thought had been that I'd put my skis on and taken off somewhere, but I'd left the sheepskin coat in the house and without a coat it seemed too crazy.

"I went to the barn and Kelly came with me. I couldn't figure what you'd be doing out there in the cold but I thought you might have thought of something else you could rig up like you did the grill and you were looking for stuff to do it with. You weren't in the barn, but your skis were in there. That told us you'd been there, but then what?"

At that point his story fell apart. If any of them was realizing it, they were saying nothing. I wasn't talking either. I just listened while he went on with it.

"When we came back out of the barn, I saw your track where you'd dragged yourself off into the woods. The new snow hadn't filled it in and covered it up yet. I couldn't figure that. It wasn't footprints. It was like you'd gone that way, dragging something after you, but it was a track and we followed it. That's how we came to find you. Otherwise you'd still be out there freezing to death."

"What was I dragging?" I asked. "Did you find anything?"

"No," Kelly said.

"We didn't look," Stan added. "Did you have anything?"

"Just myself," I said. "I remember taking my skis to the barn. I was going to put them in there. I don't remember doing it. The way I remember it, I just got as far as the barn door and that's all."

Kelly jumped in on it.

"That's where you hit your head," he said. "It wasn't there was something that tripped you up. If something trips you up, you fall forward. If you hit your head that way, it would be on your forehead, not the back of your head. What you did was slip on the snow. That's how come you fell backwards."

Stan took it up from him.

"Yeah," he said. "You're right. It wasn't that you were dragging something into the woods; you were just dragging yourself. You fell there by the barn and knocked yourself out. When you came to, you were all turned around. You couldn't stand and you tried to drag yourself back to the house, but you went dragging the other way, into the woods, till you passed out all over again."

They had finally worked it out so that it was reasonable enough. I was wondering whether I should believe it. I was pitting nothing against it but my own not too believable flashes of memory. It seemed to me that they were working too hard at piecing together a credible story, but I was fresh from a crack on the head and I was wondering how good my judgment might be.

I could have my doubts but, since I was keeping them to myself, the others seemed satisfied. They took to congratulating me on my good fortune. I'd had the same kind of accident as had finished off the old man, but I was lucky. I'd come out of it alive.

Sally asked me if I felt like eating. To my surprise, now that she had mentioned it, I did feel hungry. She had a pot of something savory bubbling away on my improvised barbecue. It was filling the room with a mouth-watering fragrance.

"I got some stew out of the freezer," she said. "The way it's cold out there tonight, it's like the whole kitchen is a deep freeze. We'll have the stew and your sandwiches and there's coffee and your doughnuts for dessert. We don't need any electricity, thanks to you."

"How's Firpo doing?" I asked.

"He's had his nice warm bottle and he's doing fine," she said.

Evidently I was in favor. I could call her kid Firpo and get away with it.

The meal was great, but cleaning up the dishes afterward took the lot of us and it took time. With the pump out, the only way we could have water was by hauling in buckets of snow to melt down and heat for the dish washing. Then there was the job of getting the room fixed for sleeping.

There were those mattresses on the floor, but there were only four mattresses for five people, even though one of them was a double. With Sally superintending, we strung a wire across the room and hung from it some big tablecloths she brought out. Since we were all going to be sleeping in our clothes, I thought she was overdoing it, but it had to be one side of the room for Mrs. Kelly and the baby and herself and the other side for Stan and Kelly and me, with the linen barrier providing at least a symbolic separation of the sexes.

"Two of you men will have to share the big mattress," she said. "You can toss for it."

"I don't care," I told her, "as long as the other guy doesn't toss on it and I don't know that I'd care even then. Nothing's going to keep me awake."

Stan settled it.

"We'll share," he told me. "You and me. After your accident, if you need anything during the night, I'll be there handy."

"Don't go sitting up watching over me," I said. "I won't need anything."

I thought I was going to have no trouble sleeping. I was beat enough for it, but there was a lot that interfered. For one thing, the room was never dark. It danced with firelight. Then there was the time when Firpo had to have his night feeding. Sally got up and was warming his bottle and Stan got up to take it away from her and send her back to sleep.

I am inclined to feel that none of that could have kept me awake, but there was my thinking. I slept and woke and slept and woke. Each time I woke, I'd start thinking again.

One of the times I looked at my watch. It was just after four, and everything had gone quiet. There was just the firelight and that had settled down to steady burning, no dancing flames. All through the room I could hear the steady breathing. Slowly and carefully I rolled off the mattress and got to my feet. I stood there awhile just waiting and listening. Nobody woke. Stan turned and, finding all that room, he sprawled across the mattress in his sleep and lay there as flat and relaxed as a rug. I picked up my boots and tiptoed out to the icy hall. Out there I put them on.

Quietly I left the house. It would be all right. If anyone woke, I could always pretend I had to go. It was colder than ever outside. The snow had stopped and there was even some moon showing through a veil of thin cloud.

I didn't have the flashlight. I had made the mistake of setting it down and the tablecloths had gone up between me and it. I didn't need it, though; I had the moonlight.

What I was going to do inside the barn would need no light. I could manage it by feel alone. I let myself into the barn and shut the door behind me. It was darker than the inside of a miser's pocket in there but I knew exactly where I would find the body lying.

I drew back the tarp and ran my hands along the body, locating the old man's pockets. I tried the right hand pants pocket first and came up with nothing that hadn't been there earlier. I tried the left hand pants pocket. I could feel the contours of the keys through the cloth even before I got my hand in. I shoved my hand in to make sure. My fingers closed over the key ring and the bunch of keys. I was fingering them, trying to identify each of them by touch. There weren't many, only five.

A sizable one, flat and grooved, would be a latchkey. Another of the same size and the same general shape would be another latchkey. He had a place in the neighborhood where he came weekends and summers. That would mean another place somewhere else for the rest of the time. Two places, two latchkeys, it worked out.

There was a very small one. Anything that size could only be a luggage key. That left the two, and nobody who had ever driven a car could have failed to know them. Larger than the luggage key but still relatively small, flat and smooth and the two very much alike, they had to be the car keys—the one for the ignition and the one for the trunk.

Now I had something solid to think about. I was just pulling my hand back out of the pocket when the light jabbed at me.

"Put your hands on top of your head and stand up slowly, mister," Stan snarled.

I knew him by his voice.

Doing as he said, I turned to face him. He had a flashlight in one hand and a revolver in the other. The revolver was aimed straight at my gut.

"Now, mister, you're going to tell me what you're up to."

I wasn't Matt any more. I was mister. He didn't have to spell it out.

It was going to be no more Mr. Nice Guy.

III

"Cool it, Stan," I said.

My words had no effect. Maybe out there in that freezing barn they were inappropriate. He kept the revolver leveled at me. He was relaxing nothing.

"Talk," he said. "And don't try to con me."

I talked.

"I woke up," I said. "I couldn't get back to sleep because there was something bugging me. I couldn't stop thinking about it."

"Like what?"

"Like his car keys. The key wasn't in the ignition. Okay. He was in the car and he didn't have the motor running, but when I found him, the car was full of gas fumes. The way we've been figuring it, he got out of the car to try to make it on foot. He fell and hit his head. So he gave up on it and went back to the car. He thought then that he could shut all the windows up tight to keep the cold out, but maybe there were enough fumes still in the car to kill him or maybe it wasn't that at all. He was an old man. Maybe it was a coronary."

"Maybe and maybe," Stan growled. "Maybe this and maybe that. So what were you doing? An autopsy starting with his pockets?"

"I was looking for his car keys," I said.

It was the truth or at least a part of it. I wasn't sure enough of him to give him the whole truth.

"What do you want with his car keys?"

"The key was out of the ignition," I said. "So where was it?"

"And?"

"I found it. It's in his pants pocket, where it ought to be."

"Where else would it be?"

"Now that I'm really awake," I said, "I realize there are all sorts of places it might have been and nothing to get worked up about. They could have dropped out of his hand. They might have been on the floor of the car or on the seat and we wouldn't have noticed."

"Or he could have lost them in the snow when he fell and hit his head," Stan suggested.

"Sure," I said. "All sorts of possibilities. I'm damned if I know why I thought it was important."

He said nothing more. He just stood there, holding the gun and the light leveled at me. It seemed a long time, but it was probably no more than the better part of a minute. I couldn't read his face. He had me spotlighted, but everything else was dark. I could see nothing but the light and the gun. Finally he spoke.

"We better get back where it's warm," he said. "Move."

I was listening for a change of tone that might have indicated some relaxation of his hostility and his suspicion. I heard none. I moved toward him, but he backed off, matching me step for step. Gesturing with the gun and the light, he turned me. He had me going out ahead of him. He was following with the gun and the light.

"All the way with my hands on my head?" I asked.

"You can stick them up your ass if you'd rather," he snarled.

I took it for a permission of sorts and I brought my hands down. I was thinking about a bullet in the back, but I told myself it wasn't likely. We were too close to the house and, if anything of that sort was coming, it would be done more subtly. The job worked on the old man had been smarter. Nothing had happened since to make a man lose his smarts.

Marching me in front of him that way, Sobieski took me back to the house. All the way into the room with the fire he kept his gun and his light on me. Once we were in there, he pocketed his flashlight. For watching me the firelight was enough. He marched me to the mattress we'd been sharing.

"All right," he growled. "Lie down."

I might have been a dog he was putting through its tricks. I got down on the mattress, taking the side I'd had before.

"Not there," he ordered. "Move over."

He was reversing our positions. He was putting himself between me and the door. I moved. Lowering himself beside me, he shoved the gun under the mattress. I could imagine it making a hard lump he wouldn't enjoy lying on, but he was putting it where I couldn't grab at it. Turning on his side, he crowded up close against me and flung his arm across my shoulders.

"You make any move, mister," he whispered, "and I'll know it."

I lay there with his hand heavy on me and his breath hitting the back of my neck. I tried to postpone thinking until the morning. I was wishing that one time or the other I had thought to check the old man's billfold. I remembered coming on what seemed a reasonable amount of change, but folding money might have been taken and the change left.

For that matter I couldn't even be certain that it had been robbery. I was remembering his words:

"He was a nice old guy. He was a good old man. Everybody liked him. He was everybody's friend."

Thinking about them, I found them taking on a new flavor. Stinker Sobieski—could he have been protesting too much? Then there had been all that urgency to get the body out of the car and take it home. Hadn't there been something irrational about that even though I had shared in the irrationality? Had that been what it seemed or had it been a great way for messing up the scene of the crime?

How about the scene of the crime? I lay there with my eyes closed and his hand heavy on my shoulder and his breath on my neck and I was trying to build it in my head, trying to see it in complete detail.

He had been covering the road on his snowmobile. He hadn't found me, I had found him, but there had been that earlier time when I was bringing the skis down from Baby's roof carrier. The snowmobile had come close and its light had been full on me, but it had turned and sped away. What had that been? He hadn't seen me and he'd decided he'd searched far enough? If he had come along the road, he couldn't have come that far without seeing the old man. If he had seen the old man, why hadn't he taken him out of the car then? Why would he go off and come back later to do it?

I tried figuring that he had seen the old man and had gone on without doing anything about him because the old man had been dead. The body had gone cold by the time I came on it. Of course, in that weather, it wouldn't have taken long for the body to go cold, but from the first time I had seen the snowmobile light to the time I found the body hadn't been that long.

So he had come on the dead old man, but his mind had been on the living. It was possible that he still had not been close enough to see me through the falling snow or to make out the contours of my car, so he went off to search in another direction.

Maybe it had been that he'd found the Kellys. I didn't know where he'd found them or when. After he'd brought them to the house, he would have been spooked by the thought of the old man dead out there in the storm. So he would have gone out again to bring the body in. Once he was out, he decided to search some more for other people stranded in other cars. For a second time he went by the dead man to explore farther along the road and this time he went as far as my car?

It wouldn't work. There was one big thing wrong: he couldn't have come from his house all the way down to where I'd left Baby to find her empty without having passed me on the road. That stopped me for a while, but I worked it out. He had already covered that stretch of road, so, when he went out again, he took another road, exploring that till it fed into the road I'd been on. That would do it. He had taken another way around to get to the old man. It would make sense for him to cover new ground on his way instead of going back and forth again and again along the same stretch of road.

It was all right as far as it went, but there still were the keys. The keys explained the attack on me: I had to be put out of the way so that they could be returned to the old man's pocket. Knocked out by the barn, I'd come to and dragged myself off into the woods only to pass out again where I could be expected to freeze to death? There was no way I could buy that.

All the same, no answer that I came up with was doing

anything for me. They were just opening up fresh questions. I was to die in the woods. Because I might have known about the keys? That wasn't good enough. Wouldn't it have been easier and safer to have gone out again on the snowmobile to lose the keys in the snow somewhere near the dead man's car?

There had to be a better reason for trying to kill Erridge. Possibly that first time the snowmobile light hit me I hadn't been invisible in the falling snow. Fresh from doing whatever he had done to the old man, he had come on me and he'd panicked. I was a witness who would put him in the area, so he turned and took off. He couldn't let me see him. Then later, when he'd calmed down, he realized that it wasn't good enough. I couldn't have failed to see his light, and he had to make sure of me. That was why the next time he had come the other way around. He was going to pick me up without going past the dead old man. We would find the body together.

He hadn't made it. When he came on Baby, she was empty. He guessed that I wouldn't have taken off back over the road I'd already covered in the car. I'd be headed in the direction of the old man. He took off after me. Since he didn't catch up with me before I'd reached the old man's car, he thought he had to stop and do something about it. Bring in the body and mess up the scene of the crime?

Bring in the body at least. It would be the only explanation he could give for having been where he was. It was another answer that wasn't good enough. He'd had what would have seemed to him a good reason for getting rid of me. He'd brought it off. I was lying in the woods. I'd be dead before anyone found me. He had it made, so why did he go right back out to search for me?

That one wasn't too hard. There was his wife and there

were the Kellys. They got to worrying. I had been out too long, and someone had to go and look for me. If he had been alone there with his wife and the baby, maybe he could have handled it with a slap in the mouth or another black eye. I couldn't buy that rake-handle story. It had been used too often.

So the answer to that one would be the Kellys. There had been too many witnesses. If he could have gone out alone, he could have not found me, but if Kelly had insisted on coming along and he hadn't been able to wait long enough for new snow to obliterate the trail he had made dragging me into the woods, he would have had no choice but to find me and bring me in.

He fell asleep. At least I thought he had because he changed position and his hand came off my shoulder. He turned so we were lying back to back and no longer touching. I wondered whether I could be sure of him. I was telling myself that it would take an unimaginable degree of cool for a man to let himself drop off in that situation.

But I felt myself dropping off too and I knew about myself. That was no kind of cool. It was simple exhaustion. Guys under enemy fire sleep in foxholes. The body can take only so much and then there's no thinking potent enough to keep it from running out on you.

There was another possibility. He could have figured out a new final solution for Matthew Erridge. He pretends he's asleep. Erridge is fooled. Erridge makes a move. He whips out the revolver and he shoots Erridge in the back. He's already caught the rat fooling around with the old man's body. He has to put a stop to that.

Maybe the hand that had been weighing down my shoulder was now under the mattress wrapped around the gun.

He'd rolled over into the best position for reaching it. I made no moves. I lay absolutely still and pretended sleep. Two, I thought, could play at that game, but then exhaustion took over. Pretense became the real thing.

It was morning when I woke. Firpo needed changing and Firpo needed a bottle. The fire needed building up. Sobieski was at the fireplace taking care of that. Sally was also up. She was looking after the baby. Kelly was still sleeping. I saw no evidence of Mrs. Kelly. She was probably behind the tablecloth barrier, resting her nerves.

The Sobieskis were whispering together. She was back to talking to him. It looked as though he had been forgiven. I yawned and stretched. Sally paid me no attention. Sobieski turned from what he was doing to the fire and scowled at me. He said nothing, but the job he had been doing on the fire went half-assed. He was no longer giving it his full attention. He wasn't taking his eyes off Erridge. He had the gun stuck in his belt.

The light coming in through the windows was gray and thin. The glass was too much frosted over to see through, but the quality of the light was discouraging. During the night I had seen the moon through a thin film of cloud. But now it looked as though we might be back under a thick cloud cover.

I shut my eyes and pretended I hadn't wakened, but behind the eyelids the old brain was up and roaring. You know how it can be when you've gone to sleep with something on your mind. You wake and it's still there but now it has come clear. That was it and I wanted a few minutes to think. I had been trying to remember every detail of the old man and his car. Now out of nowhere I had a new detail.

I was remembering the way I had first found the body.

The car had been drifted in so deep that the snow had been up over the headlights. When I'd opened the car door I'd had the wind at my back. I had opened the door on the exposed side, the side where the drifting was heaviest. When I had tried to open the door on the other side, the sheltered side, I'd found it drifted in so solidly that I hadn't been able to budge it. The door I'd opened had been easy. I hadn't needed to shovel any snow out of the way. I hadn't muscled it open. I'd just turned the door handle and opened it.

It was something I couldn't be mistaken about. If I'd had to fight the door to get at the old man's body, that would have been something I would have remembered. After all, I hadn't known whether he was alive or dead, and I'd been thinking that there was something that still could be done for him.

There was only the one way to explain it. Someone else had dug his way into that door and had freed it, and he had done it shortly before I had come on it, and it hadn't been that wizened wisp of an old man in his dying moments.

I had the picture and I had it whole. Old man Hoffman is sitting in his car, snowed in and helpless. A good neighbor comes along on his snowmobile, digs the door free, and gets Hoffman out of the car. Good neighbor will load him on the snowmobile and take him to where he can be warm and dry and fed while waiting out the blizzard. But good neighbor has other ideas. He has the old man out of the car, blips him on the head and knocks him cold. The old man falls in the snow. Good neighbor picks up the old man and puts him back behind the wheel. He rolls the windows up tight and shuts the door, leaving the old man there with the motor running. He returns when the old man is dead and he robs the body. I was kicking myself for not having checked the billfold.

Good neighbor goes off with the keys. I needed a reason for that. It could have been a mistake that he rectified later, say about the time when I got blipped on the head. That was only one possibility. I was thinking about two others. Along with the car keys on the ring there were the two latchkeys and that little luggage key. There could have been a side trip to the old man's house for additional loot. It could be a burglary and nobody to know it had been done. With the latchkey there would be no evidence of breaking and entering and with the old man dead there might be no one to know that there was anything missing.

That could explain why he'd thought it important to get the keys back into the dead man's pocket. Also there was that little luggage key. A key that small suggested something like a dispatch case or a brief case, something the old man would have had in the car with him, not big enough to lock away in the trunk, so valuable that the old man had wanted to keep it close to him. A man could have unlocked it right there by the car, but that might have seemed too dangerous. Better to take it along with the keys and go through it somewhere where it would be warm and safe.

I had begun by thinking it would have been one or the other, either the house or the old man's small and precious piece of luggage, but I was coming around to thinking it might well have been both.

When I heard Kelly's voice, I opened my eyes. Sobieski was no longer watching me and he no longer had the revolver in his belt. Kelly had the gun and, as soon as I moved, he raised the muzzle and pointed it at me. He had been delegated to guard duty while the Sobieskis were busy putting breakfast together. I knew that I wasn't going to be able to go on ignoring the gun forever, but with no immediate idea of what I was to do about it, it seemed best for the moment to play dumb on that item.

"Good morning," I said.

I made it bright and cheery. The words bounced off a wall of silence. From the look of him, Kelly just revved up his hostility a couple of notches. The Sobieskis went on with their chores. They were pretending that I hadn't spoken.

Kelly worried me. It wasn't that he looked formidable. If he had given an appearance of even being competent, I could have been more comfortable about him. He was working at looking hard and implacable, but he was a pudgy little man. What came through was only a mean and frightened look. Mean isn't good. Team it up with frightened and it becomes dangerously unpredictable. Add to all that the way he was holding the gun. Kelly had what you might call pistol hands. They were pudgy and too small for the size and weight of a revolver. I was guessing that it was the first time he'd ever held one. It was possible that he wouldn't know how to fire the thing, but it hit me as a certainty that he wouldn't know how to keep it from going off by accident.

In Sobieski's big, competent hand the revolver had been a menace. With Kelly holding it, I saw it as out of control.

It was no good pretending he wasn't there and that the gun wasn't in his hand. It was no good pretending that there could be any target anyone had in mind that wouldn't be Matt Erridge.

Play it cool, Matthew, and be damned sure you don't make any sudden moves. The fat little guy is scared. Don't do anything that might throw a worse scare into him.

"It's morning," I said. "All right if I get up?"

Kelly said nothing. Sobieski spoke.

"Let him get up," he said.

I got up slowly. I was feeling the soreness at the back of my head and I craved air. The room was shut up tight to keep the heat in and the fire had been going all night. It was a sizable room, but after five people had spent the night in it, its air smelled used.

What with the knock on my head and the stuffiness, I could make a good case for not being at the top of my form. I could pretend weakness. I could make a big thing out of the lump on my head.

I got to my feet and I wobbled a bit. I put out a hand and grabbed at a chair to steady myself. I was hoping that they would get the idea that Erridge was not in good shape and it would relax them. But Kelly showed no symptoms of relaxation.

"Okay if I go to the window?" I asked.

"What for?"

Sobieski was the only one talking to me and that no more than was necessary.

"To look out," I said. "To see how bad it looks out there."

"It's snowing again, as hard as ever. Nothing to look at."

I gathered that it wasn't all right for me to go to the window.

"My own stuff is dry by now," I said. "Anybody mind if I change back into it?"

"Why?"

"Why should anyone mind or why do I want to change?"

"Why do you want to change?"

Sobieski had dropped what he was doing. He had turned to me to ask his questions. He didn't, however, take the revolver back from Kelly.

"Your clothes are fine, Stan, and thanks for the use of them, but mine fit me better. I'm more comfortable in them."

For a moment I thought he was going to question the necessity for my feeling more comfortable, but he shrugged and turned away. He went off behind that screen of tablecloths and he came back with my pants and my shirt. He didn't hand them right over to me. First he went through the pockets, but with no show of interest in anything he was finding in them. He fastened on only one item and, though he didn't give even that much attention, he set it aside. It was the one thing I was not to be allowed. It was my pocketknife. It was the most ordinary sort of pocketknife. I could cut up an apple with it or I could whittle a stick. I'd never thought of it as a weapon.

Bundling the shirt and pants up in a ball, he tossed them at me.

"Let him change," he told Kelly. "It'll be all right."

I skinned out of the shirt and workpants he had lent me. I was just picking up my own pants to haul them on when Mrs. Kelly came around from behind the tablecloths. At sight of me, she screamed and giggled and put her hands over her eyes as she scuttled back out of sight. She had seen me in a like state of undress the night before, but no matter how often she was going to have to go into it, she was not going to give up on her little act of maidenly behavior.

Sally Sobieski went off and joined her. I could hear the buzz of their whispering—or at least of Sally's whispering—and a punctuation of little yelps of astonishment and disapproval from the Kelly dame.

Mrs. Kelly was taller than her husband and there wasn't any fat on her. The way she strutted you could tell that she was proud of her figure in that peculiar way they are when they have no figure at all, just used-looking skin stretched over their bones. Evidently she was being briefed on bad guy Erridge and why he had to be watched. I couldn't work up any sweat about that. The good opinion of Irene Kelly was never going to be among the things I needed.

I pulled on the pants and shirt and I had everything buttoned and zipped up before I spoke.

"You can come out now if you want to," I said. "I'm decent."

Nobody said anything to that, but Sally began dismantling the tablecloth barrier.

"There's bacon for breakfast," she said, "and there's oatmeal and coffee. I can't give you any milk for the oatmeal and you'll have to take the coffee black. I don't know how long we're going to be cut off and I have to keep the milk for Firpo. There's sugar though."

I took note of that "Firpo." Now that they had closed ranks against the enemy, Erridge, evidently everything was all right between her and her husband. It was obvious that she was talking to the Kellys, but I didn't have to let on that I knew it.

"Oatmeal's good," I said, "with salt and butter. Better than with cream and sugar, or it's not bad with just salt."

"There's butter," she said. "We'll have to be stuck a long time before we run out of butter. It's only the milk that's worrying me. The baby can't do without."

I took that to mean that I was to have breakfast. I hadn't been put on bread and water.

If there were to be any further comments, they were cut off. Someone was outside banging on the window. Sobieski went out. He returned carrying a back pack. He explained that Bert Dawson was out there. Dawson was taking off his snowshoes.

"More milk for Firpo," Stan was telling Sally when Dawson came into the room. "Bert's brought us all he had."

"I thought you might need it for the kid," Dawson said. "There's other stuff here, too, everything I could carry of what I had in the house. I got spooked over there all alone. No light, no heat, no telephone, no TV. Stan says it'll be all right if I join up with you folks. Okay with you, Sally?"

"Even without the milk you'd be welcome, Bert," Sally said. "But that doesn't mean I'm not grabbing the milk for Firpo."

She gave him a smile. Even with the shiner, it made her face radiantly beautiful.

Dawson was taking no notice either of me or of the revolver Kelly had leveled at me. Obviously Stan had brought him up to date on me before he brought him into the house. Dawson kept talking. He was taking a gloomy view of the weather. More snow than anyone had ever seen was already piled up and it was snowing again and as hard as before. No telling when it would stop or how much there was going to be before the weather cleared and the snowplows could come through.

"The one thing that has me going crazy is the milk," Sally said. "There's plenty of food for days and days."

"Days and days," Irene Kelly moaned. "I'll go crazy. My nerves."

"It won't be days and days," Kelly told her.

It was more a question than a statement. He was waiting for someone to say he was right. Nobody was saying it. Sally went back to talking about the food supply.

"The meals may be funny," she said, "but everybody will have enough and we can have it hot."

I was wondering whether anybody was remembering that there would have been nothing hot if Matthew Erridge, the engineering genius, hadn't rigged up the cookstove on which she had the coffee perking and the bacon sizzling and the oatmeal cooking. Then I saw that she, at least, was remembering. She shot me a quick glance. It had apology in it and doubt. As soon as our eyes met, however, she flushed and looked away.

She busied herself with the dishing up and called us to the table. Stan told me where to sit. He put me between Dawson and himself. Taking the revolver away from Kelly, he stuck it in his belt and then quickly changed the seating arrangement. Dawson had settled in on my left. Stan moved him to my right. He gave no reason for the change, but I caught it. He wasn't going to sit beside me with the gun where I might reach down and grab it. He was right-handed. He had the gun stuck in his belt on his right side.

While we were eating the oatmeal, I had an idea. It didn't seem a great idea, but it was the best I had. I thought there might be just a touch of thaw setting in. Some of the Sobieski hostility against me might have begun melting away. There was only one sign of it, if it was a sign. The Kellys took their oatmeal with sugar. The Sobieskis took it my way, with salt and butter. Watching them and me, Dawson followed suit.

"It's good this way," Stan said. "I never thought."

"Better than sugar and cream," Sally agreed.

They were speaking only to each other, but maybe they were conceding that there might be some good in me after all. Taking some small encouragement from that thought, I decided I'd make a try at my idea.

I brought out my billfold. It's well stuffed with the usual junk, credit cards, club membership cards, that sort of stuff. I had never before thought of impressing anyone with a public exhibition of it. I had actually never thought of it as being impressive, but in this situation I thought it might just possibly serve as evidence that Matthew Erridge was a solid citizen, even a man of substance. You know and I know, of course, that among the solid citizens and the men of substance might be found no few criminals but it was worth a try.

As soon as I had it in my hand, though, I knew there was something wrong with it. It wasn't as fat as it should have been. I checked it out. The credit cards, the business cards, the club membership cards were all there. What made it thinner than it should have been was the absence of two hundred bucks.

It isn't often that without counting I can give you anything more than a rough estimate of the cash I'm carrying on me, but this was one time when I could say precisely. On leaving home I had put two hundred dollars in the billfold. I had started out with that and with some change. The change was still in my pants pocket. I had taken the bills to use in places where they mightn't take credit cards and they wouldn't take my check. I had made only one stop, and that had been for gas which I paid for with a credit card.

Someone in that room had lifted the money.

IV

I'm not that mad about money. I make it and I spend it. If two hundred bucks had been the price of being picked up out of the blizzard and of being sheltered and fed in a warm, dry place while waiting for the road to open up, I'd have paid it and never thought to reckon up whether the price was moderate, fair, or excessive.

Paying, however, is one thing; having your pocket picked is another—and that, it seemed to me, was the least of it. There I was, the suspect. I was presumably to be held until I could be handed over to the law. I didn't know just how large a crime was to be charged against me, anything from attempted robbery of the dead to the big deal, murder and robbery. I couldn't be certain that one of these people holed up with me in that warm room was the murderer who killed and robbed the old man. There was, of course, the outside chance that there could have been someone else who'd been ranging the road in a snowmobile and had pulled off that crime, but on the ripoff of my two hundred bucks there was a certainty. This little group of the self-righteous, included at least one pickpocket. I wasn't ruling out the possibility of collaboration, but it was a question only of whether Erridge had fallen among thieves or had fallen afoul of a single thief.

I hadn't enjoyed being the suspect. Being both suspect and victim was too much. Meanwhile they were all watching me.

I didn't expect any of them to be looking worried or frightened. I suppose I was assuming that the one of them who had murdered and, I was certain, robbed the old man would also be the one who had dipped into my billfold. If I was right, I was up against someone who would be too cool to show anything. I was remembering that it had been Stan Sobieski who had insisted on getting me out of my wet clothes and I was now thinking for the first time that it had been behind the tablecloth screen that he had set them by the fire to dry. They could have been put just as close to the heat at the other side of the fireplace and there they would have been where I might have seen someone go through the pockets.

I studied their faces. The only one who was showing anything but hostility and suspicion was Irene Kelly. She, however, was only showing those nerves she talked about all the time. For her a flutter of agitation was normal. Maybe she looked calm in her sleep, but about that I didn't know. Asleep she had been screened from me.

"Okay," Sobieski growled. "What is it?"

"Two hundred bucks," I said.

"What about two hundred bucks?"

"They were in my billfold."

I held it spread open for them to see.

"You saying you had two hundred bucks and somebody ripped you off?"

"I'm saying I had two hundred bucks and now I don't have them."

"You're accusing somebody here?"

"I started out yesterday with two hundred dollars. I made one stop. That was for gas and I paid with a credit card. That was the only time I had the billfold out of my pocket. When I put it back in my pocket at the gas station, it still had the two hundred in it. I didn't look at the money then. I didn't count it, but the billfold was fat. When I took it out for the second time, and that was only just now, it was thinner in my hand than it had been. You can see for yourself. It's thinner by five twenties and ten tens."

"If they ever were in there," Kelly said.

"Right," I told him. "You have only my word for it that it was two hundred, but you should have your own common sense to tell you that it would have been something. Can you believe that I went riding along without even one buck on me?"

"You've got a couple of bucks," Sobieski said. "I saw when I checked you for weapons. You've got more than two dollars in change."

"You counted it?" I asked. "Is that what you had it out of my pants pocket for?"

It was a good question even though it might not have been smart to ask it. He had the gun and he'd been looking hostile, but I was too angry to think about that. Without thinking about it, however, I was foreseeing moves and measuring distances. What would be coming I didn't know, but I had not the slightest doubt but that it was going to be ugly.

But then it wasn't. He reacted. It was inevitable that he should, but it was the one reaction I hadn't been foreseeing. It caught me off base.

He flushed. He stammered. If I had been looking for someone to come up with a guilty look, I had it right there, but all it was giving me was confusion. It was just too out of line with the rest of his performance. On everything before this he had been ready with his answers and then he'd had every reason for thinking he could ride along without any possibility of being questioned.

Now, when it was obvious that he couldn't have not known the question would come up, he was fumbling for an answer. I tried to understand that. I could only think he had been so confident that he had me cowed that he'd expected I wouldn't have the guts to ask the question.

"I put your pants to dry," he said. "The change fell out of your pocket. I gathered it up off the floor and put it back."

"Counting it as you went just to make sure it wasn't worth taking?"

I was pushing. If you think I was being foolhardy, you're leaving out the intangibles. Suddenly I was having the feeling that all of the toughness had gone out of him. It even seemed possible that I had the guy on the run. It was one of those things you can never pin down. You just sense it, but I'd never been more certain of anything. His assurance was gone. He was shaken.

"I was looking to see maybe I could find something you'd swiped off the old man's body," he said.

Those were hardly the words of an apology, but the tone was apologetic. The man was sick with shame. It showed all over him. Also with every word he was saying, he was making admissions. He had been trying to find something I might have stolen from the old man's body. Certainly he wouldn't have checked out that one pocket where I keep my change and have left it at that. Nothing could have been more unlikely. He was as good as admitting that he had been through all my pockets apart from the time when he had done it before me and had removed the pocketknife. Certainly that other inspection would have included the billfold. I had him at a disadvantage. I pushed on.

"Did you find anything?" I asked.

"No," he said. "I didn't find anything."

He had broken out in a sweat. I could smell it on him. I was telling myself that I'd be a fool to let up on him now. There was no reason to be sorry for him and, even if there had been a reason, I couldn't afford it. Remembering something, I had an even sharper picture of how much he was rattled. At the very start of these questions of mine, he'd had an easy out and he'd been too shaken to use it.

He could have reminded me that he had been through my pockets in my presence. I had seen him handle the change then.

At that point Kelly jumped in to help him.

"What's to say he didn't take the two hundred out of his wallet himself if he ever had two hundred?" he said. "Whatever he had in bills he could have taken it out of there himself just so he could yell he was robbed."

It was feeble, but I was expecting that Sobieski would grab at it. In a spot like that a man snatches at straws. He didn't snatch.

"No," he said. "You were watching him when I gave him back his stuff. We all been watching him ever since. We saw right off when he took his wallet out."

"Like they say," Kelly insisted, "the hand is quicker than the eye."

"And the mouth is quickest of all," I told him.

"Don't get fresh with me, mister," Kelly blustered. "I don't take any lip from the likes of you."

"Watch it, little fat man," I said. "You might be taking a thick lip from the likes of me."

Irene Kelly put a restraining hand on her husband's arm. It was a superfluous hand. He was making no moves. Maybe she liked to think she had a tiger there and she had to keep him tamed.

"Please, Michael," she wailed. "Don't even talk to him."

"He threatened me. You all heard it. You heard him threaten me."

"Please, Michael. My nerves. Please."

Her husband shot her a look that told her what she could do with her nerves. What he said, however, was addressed to the company at large.

"It didn't have to be when I was watching him," he said.

"Then it would have been when I was watching him and then he was wearing my stuff, not his," Sobieski said. "His stuff was drying and he was never anywhere near it."

"What about before?" Kelly persisted.

"I've been through all his pockets. He hasn't any money anywhere on him, except the change."

Sobieski was standing his ground.

"Before that," Kelly said. "He could have left his money in his car."

Sally Sobieski broke in on it.

"I don't like this," she said. "This is my house and I won't stand for it in my house."

"Anyhow," Sobieski said, "it's nonsense. Why would he leave his money in his car and then say he's been robbed?"

"Just so he could say that," Kelly argued. "Just so he could pretend he's the one that's got a complaint."

"That's enough," the lady of the house told him. "Nobody's going to say another word about this. I won't have it and I'm not fooling. We're stuck here, all of us, until the road's opened up. We have to live together and we're going to live together in peace. This is my house and that's the way it's going to be. Anybody who can't behave himself can just get out and that goes for all of you."

"Everybody but Firpo," Sobieski said.

"Don't make a joke of it, Stan," his wife snapped. "I'm not kidding."

"Sally's right," he said. "We're none of us kidding. Somebody's taken Matt's money."

"If you're going to believe him . . ." Mrs. Kelly began.

"I believe him," Sobieski said.

"Then you're saying one of us is the thief even though you know he's the thief," Mrs. Kelly went on. "You caught him at it yourself."

"I don't know what I caught him at," Sobieski growled. "Anyhow that has nothing to do with this. This happened here in the house. Sally doesn't like it and I don't like it. It's our house. We've got the right to say what goes on here. Somebody took his money. Somebody's going to give it back."

Kelly gave out with a sneering laugh.

"Just like that," he said.

"Just like that," Sobieski said.

He pulled the revolver out of his belt. For a moment I thought he might be having the crazy idea of pointing it at someone and saying, "Stand and deliver." I was even wondering who he would choose. I was wrong.

Holding the gun out where we could all see it, he unloaded it and dropped the shells into his pocket. Pointing it at the ceiling, he squeezed the trigger six times, sending the hammer home on each of the empty chambers. Having completed his demonstration, he took the revolver to a cabinet and locked it away. The key he dropped into the pocket where he had stored the ammo.

Sally's eyes misted and she smiled. She went over to him and kissed him.

"Thank you," she said.

Sobieski put his arm around her and, holding her close

against him, he outlined for us the procedure he was demanding.

"Each one of us is going to go out to the hall," he said. "We'll go one by one with nobody out there to watch us and nobody to see anything. That'll give the one who has the money the chance to bring it out and hide it in his hand."

He paused and looked around the room. After a moment, he fastened on a big canvas bag that hung alongside the fireplace. It was something he used for bringing logs in for the fire.

"That bag there," he said. "Each one, when he comes back in, will have his hand in a tight fist. There'll be something in it or there'll be nothing in it. Nobody'll know that but him. He will go straight to the bag and bury his fist in it. Then the next one will go out to the hall and do the same thing. The money will be in the bag and nobody will know who put it there."

"And that'll finish it," Sally said. "We'll hear no more about it."

Glowering, Kelly pointed a finger at me.

"Him, too," he said.

"Everybody," Sobieski told him. "Him, me, Sally. Like I said before, everybody but Firpo."

"His fist's too small," I said.

"And he can't reach up far enough to get into anyone's pocket," Sobieski added.

Sally gave us both a beautiful smile, and I even was getting something like a friendly grin from Stan. I could see that my acquiescence to their plan for settling the matter of my money without further unpleasantness was winning me points with the Sobieskis.

"And not Bert," Sally said. "He's out of it, too."

Dawson laughed.

"I've got a big fist," he said, "and I can reach."

"You weren't here when Stan took the pants off me," I said. "You weren't here any time when I didn't have them on."

"I've been missing all the fun," Dawson said.

Sobieski evidently didn't like that line of talk. He broke in on it.

"Let's quit kidding around," he said. "Let's get this over with."

"Who goes first?" Irene Kelly asked.

"You, Mrs. Kelly," Stan said.

"Why me?"

"Ladies first, so it's you and Sally and you're the guest."

"I want Michael to go out with me."

"No." Stan had laid down the rules. "No. Everybody goes out alone."

"I'm afraid," the woman whimpered. "I'm afraid alone."

"There's nothing to be afraid of," Sally told her.

"That old man thought there was nothing to be afraid of, didn't he?"

Stan sighed.

"All right," he said. "I'll go out with you. I'll show you that nobody's there. I'll lock and bolt the front door so nobody can come in and then you won't have to be afraid to be out there alone for the minute or two it will take."

"Take for what?" she asked.

"To take the money from wherever you have it and hide it in your fist," he said patiently.

"You're saying I have it," Irene Kelly screamed. "I don't have to take that. I don't have to take it from you or from anybody else."

"We're all in this together," Stan said. "If you think I'm accusing you, then I'm accusing myself just as much and my wife and everybody else. I'm accusing nobody and I'm accusing everybody. I don't know any other way to do it."

"I've got nerves, terrible nerves and nobody cares," the Kelly woman screamed. "I'm not going to stay out there alone, not even for a second, not with all those other rooms where someone could be hiding and waiting."

Sally looked as though she wanted to shake the woman. When she spoke, her throat tensed with the effort it took for her to hold her voice low. She was fighting down her natural desire to scream at the impossible Mrs. Kelly.

"Hiding and waiting and frozen to death," she said. "At least so stiff with the cold he couldn't move."

"I don't care. My nerves. I'd go crazy."

"All right," Stan shouted. I'll take you through the whole house. You're going with me and I don't give a damn how cold you get. We'll go through all the rooms. You can look in the closets and under the beds and then I'm going to leave you alone out there in the hall. You don't have to stay there more than a moment or two, but you're going to do it."

Sally tried to help.

"I'll go first," she said. "That'll show you it's all right."

She went out and after a moment she returned with her fists buried in the pockets of her dress. Without taking them out of her pockets she went to the canvas bag. Standing at the bag with her back to us so that we couldn't see her hands when she brought them out and plunged them into the bag, she went through the required motions and then turned back to us with her hands spread open.

"See," she said. "It's easy. That's all there is to it."

"That's right," Stan said. "We all do it exactly the way

Sally did. We just put our hands in the bag and open them. We don't go all the way down in. We don't feel for anything in the bottom. Nobody checks on who puts the money back. We want to wipe it out and forget it and this is the only way."

He turned to Mrs. Kelly.

"I want Michael with me," she whimpered.

"While I lock the door," Stan said, "and while you check the rest of the house if you still want to. If you're going to do that, though, take your coats. You're going to be mighty cold."

From the look of her, smug satisfaction was tamping down the famous Kelly nerves. She had won that small skirmish and her victory appeared to be doing therapeutic miracles for her. She picked up her coat and handed it to her husband, waiting for him to help her into it. He did what was expected of him but not without an exasperated grimace behind her back. He shrugged into his own coat.

She had a bag with her. I don't mean her handbag. She had that, too, but this was a suitcase. She picked it up and handed it to Kelly to carry for her. I would have thought that she was taking it with her because she had my two hundred stowed in it, but I'd noticed that the Kellys never made even the slightest move without lugging that suitcase with them.

Stan herded them out to the hall, careful to shut the door behind him. He was keeping the heat in.

"The pride she takes in those nerves of hers," Sally said. "You'd think she invented them."

"What's to say she didn't?" I asked.

"What I don't get," Dawson muttered, "is how her husband stands her, how any man can stand that all the time."

"I don't know," Sally said. "After all, she can stand him.

It's a good marriage. They could have spoiled two families."

They were gone a considerable time. Evidently the lady was insisting on the full inspection of the cold rooms. In due course, however, Stan pushed the door open and Kelly came dashing in to make a beeline for the fire. He had the suitcase with him. Through the briefly opened door we could hear Mrs. Kelly's wailing.

"I'm cold," she was screaming. "I'm half dead of the cold."

"Your own fault," Stan barked at her, as he came in and shut the door behind him.

Almost immediately afterward, she pushed it open and came running in with her hands buried in her coat pockets. Her teeth were chattering and the tears were running down her cheeks. She made straight for the fire and shouldered her husband aside to plant herself squarely in front of it. She started to pull her hands out to warm them at the fire. Before she had more than started the motion, Stan was on her. Grabbing her forearms from behind, he hauled down on them so hard that he all but forced her fists through the bottoms of her pockets. Holding her that way, he marched her to the canvas bag.

"The bag first," he said. "Then you can warm your hands."

"You and your silly bag," she snarled. "I haven't anything to put into it."

She went through the charade nevertheless and only then Stan let go of her. She hurried back to the fire and warmed her hands.

Stan turned to me.

"Now you, Matt," he said.

I started for the door. Kelly jumped past me and stationed

himself with his back to it, barring my way. I wanted nothing more than to grab him by the scruff of the neck and pick him up and set him to one side, but I was telling myself that this was Stan Sobieski's show, and I had to wait for him to call it. Since I also wanted to see how he was going to call it, I didn't too much mind waiting.

"He can't go out there alone," Kelly said. "What if he takes off?"

"Where'll he take off to in this blizzard?" Stan asked.

"There's your snowmobile out there. He takes it and he's gone."

"He wouldn't be gone far," Stan said. "It's about out of gas. If there's enough left in it for a couple of hundred yards, that's the most."

Dawson made a face.

"At least you had some," he said. "The storm caught me without any. I couldn't even get mine started."

"Are you sure? No gas?"

Kelly wasn't satisfied.

"You think I'd just be sitting here with the worry about Firpo's milk if there was enough gas to get me to town?"

"Still."

Kelly was reluctant to give way.

"Step aside and let him through," Stan ordered. "I want to get this over with."

Kelly stepped aside. As I opened the door and went out to the hall, I could hear him going on with it.

"You all heard me," he was saying. "I warned you. Nobody can say I didn't warn you."

I stayed out only a moment. He was still warning them when I came back in. I walked past him with my fists in my pants pockets.

"You haven't much time to shut up," I told him, "only until I can take my hands out of my pockets."

Whether it was the threat that did it, I don't know. I'd been out and back. It could have been the realization that there was no further sense in warning them that made him stuff the cork in it. Either way he fell silent. I crossed to the canvas bag, and, following Stan's instructions to the letter, I went through the motions. After that it went quickly. Kelly went out and came back and went to the bag.

Stan was the last to go. When he lifted his hands out of the canvas bag, he took it off the hook, carried it to the table, upended it, and shook it. Nothing fell out but some dust and a few bits of bark, which had been clinging to the canvas.

"That proves it," Irene Kelly said. "I knew it all along."

"Proves what?"

"There never was any two hundred dollars. It was crazy to believe him."

"No crazier than not believing him," Stan said.

Dawson, aloof from the whole thing, could be amused.

"Now what do you do?" he asked. "Strip everybody and search them?"

If Stan Sobieski had a sense of humor, he had stowed it away for the duration. He just stood there scowling.

"Let's just drop it," I said. "Tens and twenties all look alike unless you have a record of the serial numbers, and who does that? I know I don't. So somebody has two hundred bucks. What's to say it's my two hundred?"

"See?" Irene Kelly said. "I knew it. He's backing off. That proves it."

Stan rounded on her.

"That proves shit," he growled.

Jumping at the word, she went all high and mighty about

it. Nobody used that kind of language to her. She was a lady, and she expected to be treated like a lady.

"You want to wash my mouth out with soap?" Stan asked her. "Or are you thinking you'll get your husband to do it?"

She looked to Kelly. She was waiting for him to take up the cudgels for her. Squirming under her gaze, he made a feeble stab at it.

"You ought to apologize to the ladies," he mumbled.

Sally stepped into it.

"Stan isn't apologizing to anybody," she said. "It's Matt's money and he says to drop it. I don't like it and neither does Stan, but there's nothing we can do about it except pray that they get the road open soon so that you won't have to stay here with us common people."

"You said it. I didn't," Mrs. Kelly screamed. "You heard the word he used to me."

"I heard it," Sally screamed back at her. "He used that word and he uses other words and I use them too. Words don't pick pockets."

"You're accusing us?"

"Since you ask me, Mrs. Kelly," Sally told her, "I'm accusing you. You're the only one here who had even a minute alone when you could get at Matt's billfold. You and I were over there together all night. There was no time when I could have touched anything of his without your seeing me, but there were times when you could have done it. I was up during the night fixing the baby's bottle. You were alone for plenty of time then. Also this morning when I got up to take care of him and to fix breakfast, you had a lot of time alone. Were you asleep all that time, Mrs. Kelly? For a woman with your nerves are you that good a sleeper? Stan gave you a chance to get yourself out of it with nobody saying anything, but you wouldn't take it. All right, you've got Matt's two hundred dollars and we all know it, so you might be smart not to get so high and mighty with us around here."

Mrs. Kelly burst into tears. She wracked her body with wild sobs. Between sobs she sputtered. She had never been so insulted; she and her husband were never going to speak to any of us again; none of us were to speak to her. She never thought she'd see the day when anyone would take the word of a proven thief against her, Irene Kelly, who didn't have a dishonest bone in her body.

Her caterwauling woke Firpo and the kid started yelling. Stan picked him up and worked at quieting him. Sally laced into Irene Kelly and all her honest bones.

"Don't be a fool," she said. "You're going to have to stay here till the road's cleared. There's no help for that. If we can put up with you, you can put up with us; but there's one thing you better know. You woke my baby and you scared him. You're not going to do that again. You even raise your voice around here another time and I'll give you something to scream about. Remember that. I've had all that I'm going to take from you."

That did it. The woman cowered away from Sally and dodged behind her husband. She returned to her recurrent theme, but Sally had made her point. Irene Kelly was holding it down to a just barely audible mumble.

Having disposed of her, Sally was ready to take on Firpo. Stan had gentled him to the place where he had stopped crying. Sally worked at lulling him back to sleep.

Stan and I cleaned up the breakfast stuff and Dawson lent a hand. The Kellys had withdrawn. They hadn't moved off so far that they were away from the warmth of the fire but far enough to establish that they were distancing themselves from the rest of us. It was okay with me, and none of the others seemed to be having any regrets over this token separation. Everyone was waiting for the time when it could be more than token.

I went out with Stan to bring in the buckets of snow we needed for dishwashing water. It gave me a few minutes alone with him.

"Thanks for believing me about the two hundred," I said.

"I had to believe you."

"You didn't have to. I appreciate it that you did."

"I had to," he repeated. "At first when you brought it up, I was confused. Look, I was sure you took something off the old man's body. I went through everything you had on you, and I didn't find anything that couldn't have been yours. There was the money, of course, and no way of telling about that except that the old man did have money on him and it's there in his wallet. I couldn't figure out why you'd have left some, but anyhow I saw what you had in your wallet. It was two hundred in tens and twenties, just like you said. When we got to talking about it, I remembered I'd seen it."

"Why didn't you say that inside?" I asked. "When you remembered, why didn't you say anything?"

He shrugged.

"It was gone," he said, "and who was to say I didn't take it myself? When Sally told her off, she left me out of it, but you know and I know I'm not out of it. It's the Kelly dame or me. Nobody else could."

V

"Not you," I said.

"Thanks, but why not?"

"A couple of reasons," I said. "You didn't have to tell me you'd seen the two hundred. You didn't have to back me up. You could have left it that I was a liar and trying to pull a fast one."

"Uhhuh. What else?"

"You'd have to be all kinds of a fool to steal the money when you could have had it honestly. You brought me into the house. You're providing food and lodging. You can charge for it. As a matter of fact, you should."

"When?" he asked. "Before I hand you over to the police or after?"

"You are handing me over to the police?"

He shrugged.

"I've got to tell them about you and old man Hoffman's body," he said. "The old man was in the diamond business. He could have been carrying diamonds. Lots of times he did. Maybe not always, but lots of times. He didn't have any on him, but maybe he had them in the car. I left you there and instead of following me, like you said you would, you went back to your own car."

He didn't have to spell out the rest of it. At best it might be that after he'd gone off with the body, I'd looked the car over and found the diamonds. Since he knew I didn't have any on me, he was considering the possibility that I picked up the diamonds and made the trip back to Baby to stow them away there.

That way, he would be figuring me for a guy who robbed the dead. But that would be only the least of it. He could be thinking that I had killed the old man and that, when he left me by the old man's car, I already had the diamonds on me. I would have made the jaunt back to Baby to stow them there rather than risk having them on me when he took me home with him. I had, after all, urged him to take the body in first.

I can't say I liked any of this, but I had to admit to myself that the man had a point. If I felt that I had grounds for being suspicious of him, he had equal grounds for these suspicions of me.

Eventually the roads would be cleared and the two cars would be dug out. The old man's car would be checked for diamonds. If none were found, my car would be searched. Whether the police would want to hold me then—I was certain, of course, that they would find Baby clean—was going to depend on how credible they would consider my explanation of what I'd been doing in the old man's pockets.

I wasn't worrying about the police. My problem, as I saw it, was going to be staying alive until I could go to them or until I was handed over to them. Maybe Stan Sobieski wasn't hinting at murder, but I couldn't be certain. Whichever way he was thinking, one thing was for sure. My own thoughts were yelling murder. The old man hadn't had an accident. He had been killed.

I was certain. Once I'd remembered how easily that one door of the snowed-in car had opened, I could no longer have any doubts. His killer had tried it again with me. He'd failed then but not by much. He'd come too close and I could expect that he would try again.

We returned to the house, and had just finished with the dishwashing when the telephone rang. The thing had been dead along with the power lines, but now service had been restored. Sobieski grabbed it up. It was our first word from outside. The repair crews were out. Electric power had already been restored to part of the area, and we could hope it would be coming our way before long.

While Sobieski was relaying this news to us, he was busily dialing. He got through to the local dairy. They had milk. Even though the farmers hadn't been able to bring any in since the roads closed down, the dairy still had all the milk that had come in just before the storm, but they had no way to distribute it.

Sally bit hard on her lip but she couldn't stop the tears that came brimming out of her eyes. She dashed them away with the back of her hand, but they kept coming.

Stan dialed another number.

"We're not licked," he told her. "Somebody around here must have a snowmobile with a full tank or has it some place where he can get it filled. I'll find someone to run milk out to us."

It was an idea, but he was getting nothing but busy signals. He dialed again and again.

"Who are you calling?" Sally asked. Her voice was small and tremulous.

"Police barracks," Stan answered. "They can do it or they'll get through to someone who can on an emergency like this. If I can get through to them."

Irene Kelly forgot about the distance the Kellys had been

putting between themselves and the rest of us. She stormed at Sobieski.

"You better be careful," she said. "I know what you're up to. You won't get away with it. We'll sue you."

She was all over him, clawing at his hand, trying to pull it away from the dial. He shouldered her off. Even though there was weight and power behind that shoulder, it didn't look to be enough to send her sprawling. If you ask me, when she went down, she was working at making the most of the shove.

"He hit me," she screamed. "You saw it. He hit me."

Sitting on the floor at his feet, she screamed her threats up at him. He ignored her and kept dialing the police number over and over.

"If anyone's going to bring charges," she screamed.

As was to have been expected, she woke Firpo and the kid added his yowls to hers. Sally turned on her and smacked her. It was a good, hard slap. It shocked her into momentary silence. Sally turned away and picked up the baby, and I took over.

I grabbed the Kelly dame by the arm and hauled her to her feet. "If anyone's going to bring charges," I told her, "I'm the one to do it. So shut up and behave yourself."

She tried to pull free. She turned to her husband, but he wasn't moving. Letting go of her, I shoved her at him. He took her by the arm and moved her away from the rest of us. He was re-establishing the distance they had been putting between us.

I turned to Stan.

"You've got a car and a pickup in the barn," I said.

"They're no good in this."

"I know that," I told him, "but how are they for gas?"

"Empty. I siphoned the gas out of them when I was running low for the snowmobile and now that's about used up."

"Enough to get us back to Hoffman's car and mine?"

"Not nearly. Anyhow what for?"

All the time he was dialing and getting busy signals. It was obvious. People all over the place were having emergencies or they thought they were. Everybody and his uncle were calling that police number.

"For gas," I said. "The old man may not have run out. I know I didn't. There's at least a half a tank in mine. We can run over on the snowmobile as far as it will go, and I can make it the rest of the way on my skis. All I need is an empty gas can and the hose. I'll siphon out a can of gas and bring it back to you and the snowmobile."

He gave up on the dialing. I had him listening to me.

"With that," I said, "we'll have enough to carry us all the way to my car again and we can fill you up. That will get you to where you can pick up the milk and a good supply of gas."

Sally's tears dried up. Stan broke out in a grin. Across the space they'd put between us, Irene Kelly spoke up.

"Look," she said, "he's going to trust that man."

Stan turned to Dawson.

"How are you fixed, Bert?" he asked.

"For gas? I told you I ran out. The storm caught me with the snowmobile tank dry as a bone."

"Your pickup? That couldn't have been empty. Did you siphon it out for the snowmobile or have you got some in the tank?"

Dawson looked sheepish.

"I never thought of siphoning it," he said. "I've been going back and forth on the snowshoes."

Sobieski turned to me. The grin was now lighting up his whole face.

"We're in, Matt," he said. "There's maybe enough left in the snowmobile for across the fields to Bert's place. What we'll get out of his pickup should take us all the way to your car at least. You can forget the skis."

Stan was grabbing up his hat and gloves and climbing into his padded jacket. I picked up my sheepskin.

"It won't take two guys," Dawson said.

"It might," I argued. "If your gas is too low, we might still need the skis."

"I'll go," Dawson offered. "If my gas is too low, I can do it snowshoeing."

That had me stopped. I was trying to figure out a good answer to it. If anyone was going, I wanted it to be Matt Erridge. There were things I had to see.

Stan took care of it for me.

"You've been out," he said. "Back and forth on the snowshoes. We've been cooped up. We need the air."

"My garage is locked," Dawson said.

"Okay, so hand over the keys. I promise you we won't steal your pickup. We can't drive it anywhere."

This was a new Stan Sobieski. I'd given him the lift he needed. Now everything was a laugh; nothing could get him down.

Dawson brought out his keys. He fumbled around trying to work the garage key off the ring. Stan was impatient.

"Don't bother with that," he said. "Give me the lot. I'll bring them back."

"Keep your pants on," Dawson growled. "I'll have it off in a minute."

Stan laughed.

"Don't trust me?" he said.

Dawson wasn't laughing.

"You lose them in the snow and then where am I?" he mumbled.

Stan stopped laughing.

"I never knew you were such an old woman," he said.

Dawson told him to go screw. This time the Kelly woman didn't cover her ears or make a fuss. Words weren't bothering her now. She had other things on her mind.

Dawson seemed to be forever over it, but finally he had the garage key separated from the ring. He handed it to Stan.

"I'll guard it with my life, Bert," Stan told him. "I promise you I won't lose it."

His high spirits had returned.

We started out and Sally came with us. Out in the cold hall with the door shut behind us, she threw her arms around Stan and kissed him. He came away from it beaming.

"Nice," he said. "Very nice, but, after all, he's my kid, too."

She stuck her tongue out at him and turned to me.

"That's right," she said. "He isn't Matt's kid."

With that she put her arms around me and kissed me. I can't say she put quite as much into it as she had in the one she gave Stan, but I'm not knocking it. I enjoyed it, but I didn't know how much I ought to let it show. To conceal it might seem ungrateful. To let it hang out might not go down too well with the lady's husband.

It went down all right. He was still grinning.

"After that," he said, "I have to take you with me. Not a chance I'll go off and leave you here with her."

Sally pushed us toward the door.

"Get moving, you fools," she said.

We moved.

We made a brief stop in the barn to pick up the hose we were going to need for the siphoning and a couple of empty gas cans he had out there.

"That's a wonderful family you have," I said. "Good wife, beautiful kid."

"Yeah," he mumbled. "Ever since we been married I couldn't believe my luck. But today I got to thinking maybe my luck was running out. This storm and worrying about the milk. It was my fault and she could have told me it was, but she never said a word even though she's been going crazy with the worry."

That was a puzzler. I could figure no way it could have been his fault—certainly not the storm. By the time he'd said it, we were loading on to the snowmobile. Before I could say anything, we'd started off and, while we were blasting along, talk was impossible. He had been right about the gas. Those things cover ground but, before we'd covered much of it, there was the coughing and the sputtering and we stood dead in the snow.

I strapped on the skis, coiled the siphoning hose in the pocket of my coat, and lashed one of the gas cans to my back. While I was getting ready, he was giving me directions. The snow was falling heavily, but it wasn't quite as thick as it had been the day before. Now there was some visibility.

He pointed out a clump of trees ahead and slightly to the left. They were evergreens and they were easy to see. I was to head straight for those trees. Once I passed them, I would see the house and the garage.

"Straight on," he said, "and it's about a hundred yards past the trees. If you are quick, you can follow your own ski track back to here."

"I won't get lost," I told him. "I'll head back to the trees. They'll give me the direction and it's a straight line."

"Everything I do is stupid," he fretted. "I could have taken snowshoes. I didn't think."

"I'll be okay," I said. "You're getting a habit of blaming yourself for everything. You don't think you blew up this blizzard?"

"Not the snow," he said. "The milk. I should have thought to save gas for some emergency. If Firpo got sick or we ran out of milk . . . I just didn't think. I had to go and burn up the gas even though she didn't want me to."

I pushed off, wishing I could understand the guy. He seemed simple enough and straightforward, a good husband and a good father, trying to do his best for his wife and kid. More than that, he was the good neighbor who went out to rescue people from their snowed-in cars. It seemed strange that a guy like that should go on the way he was, acting as though he were laboring under some load of guilt. It didn't seem as though he could have it in him to put on any big act, and yet I couldn't be sure.

I tried to tell myself that he had reason enough to be suspicious of me, maybe even as much reason as I had for being suspicious of him, but I couldn't make it stick. I was the one who had been blipped on the head. I had been hauled off into the woods and left there to freeze to death. He hadn't. All he had against me was catching me with my hand in the dead man's pocket. I was wondering whether he could have found that so bad in itself. It seemed to me that he was overreacting. If catching me as he had, however, told him that I was on to something and if what I might find was dangerous to him, then I could hardly call it overreacting.

Thinking about it was getting me nowhere. It just left me

wishing that he didn't seem such a decent sort of guy. Everything I'd actually seen him do and everything he said served only to confuse me. Telling me that the old man had been in the diamond business and might have been carrying stones around with him seemed like something he didn't have to do and yet I wondered whether his coming out with that was as ingenuous as he'd made it sound. After all, once we were back in touch with the outside world, it would come out. Obviously it was common knowledge. Telling me about it could lose him nothing, while it served to build up his look of innocence.

I made it to the clump of trees and it was as he had promised. Coming past the trees, I saw the house ahead and beyond it the garage. I had to pass the house to get to the garage. The way the place was all mantled with snow you couldn't tell too much about it, but it didn't have the well-kept look of the Sobieski place. That, I told myself, could be the difference between the man who lives alone and the man who's making a home for his wife and child.

I pushed past the house to the garage. I had been thinking that once I was out of the snow, I might allow myself a couple of puffs on a cigarette, but as soon as I'd unlocked the garage door and had pulled it open, I knew I was going to have to forget it. The place stank of gasoline.

The fumes were so heavy in there that I thought we could be in trouble. Maybe Dawson took no better care of his pickup truck than he did of his house. If the gas in the tank of the pickup had all leaked away and there would be nothing to refuel the snowmobile, I could make it back to the Sobieski place on my skis, but Stan would be stranded out in the middle of nowhere. It would take time before I could get back to the house and return to him with snowshoes and that much time we wouldn't have, not with the temperature standing where it was. The guy would freeze before I could get back to him.

I uncapped the pickup's gas tank and set to work at siphoning gas. I dropped the hose into the tank and, when I sucked on it to start the flow, I did something I don't often do. I thanked whatever powers there might be up there above the snow clouds. There was gas in the tank. I filled the can and I was careful not to lose a drop.

The siphoning, of course, added to the stink of the gas fumes, but I'd left the garage door open and enough air was coming in to hold it down. I capped the can and hoisted it on my back. I left the garage door open because we'd be coming right back to it. It would be safe enough and it did need airing out. Dawson didn't have to know.

With the weight of the filled gas can on my back it was slower going. I found Stan. He was jumping up and down to keep his blood moving but the little I could see of him past the scarf he had wrapped around his head was blue with cold.

We emptied the can of gas into the snowmobile tank. Then it was a quick run to Dawson's garage. Once we were inside Stan hurried to shut the garage door. I didn't notice that it made it any warmer in there, but I suppose it seemed warmer to Stan.

All the time we were siphoning the rest of the gas out into the snowmobile tank, he was cursing Dawson. If the fool hadn't gone to all that trouble taking the garage key off his key ring, we would have had the key to his house. We could have gone in there and built ourselves a fire. Now that we knew we had gas, there was no great need for hurry. We could have stopped long enough to get Stan warmed up before we started out again. Stan needed it. He was shivering uncontrollably. His teeth were chattering.

I did the siphoning. Shaking with cold, Stan wasn't good for much and it was important to work carefully. We couldn't afford to lose any of the precious stuff. I came to the bottom of the pickup truck and I tried the snowmobile. It got us nothing. Dawson hadn't exaggerated: the snowmobile tank was dry.

"You've got to go and get warm," I told Stan.

He insisted that he'd be all right, but I told him that he wasn't. On the skis I had gotten enough action to keep me warm, but he would be no better sitting on the snowmobile than he had been standing and waiting for me. If anything, it would be worse for him then. I wanted him to blast himself back to his place, give himself a good slug of booze, and stay by the fire.

"I can make it out to the cars on my skis," I said. "I can hang both the gas cans on my shoulders and bring them back to you filled. By that time you'll be in shape to take off for the milk."

"No," he insisted. "I'll be okay. We'll go together."

"You think I won't come back?" I said. "You think I'll take off and ski all the way to the border and disappear into Canada?"

He didn't answer that. Maybe he didn't want to and maybe there was a limit to the number of words he could get out past his chattering teeth.

"We'll go together," he repeated.

We couldn't stand there forever arguing in that freezing garage.

I shrugged it off.

"All right," I said. "Back to your house. We'll go out again after you've warmed up."

He was satisfied with that. We took off. I stopped to lock the garage door behind us. It was a silly thing to do, but it was Dawson's garage and Dawson wanted it that way. The run back was quick, but the way Stan was shaking, it didn't seem quick enough.

Back at the house, after one look at her man, Sally took over. She pushed him close to the fire. I poured him a good slug of whiskey and took one for myself.

Dawson asked how well we'd done. I told him that we'd made it to his place and had taken all his gas. I explained that we hadn't been able to do more because we had to get Stan back to warm him up. I let myself go into complete detail about that having been necessary since we hadn't been able to warm ourselves at Dawson's place. I'd expected that he would at least say he was sorry but he just took it as though it had to be that way.

"You've got my garage key?" he asked, and that was all he said.

I handed him the key and he busied himself with working it back on to his key ring. I was learning to dislike the guy. I have nothing against old women, but an old woman with balls is hard to take.

Meanwhile Sally was mixing a lot of cocoa into boiling water. She poured it into two mugs, stirred in a heap of sugar, and laced the two mugs well with whiskey.

"Drink that, both of you," she ordered. "There's nothing better for warming you up."

It was sickeningly sweet, but she was right about its effect. It sent a great warmth coursing all the way through me. Stan came around to looking like himself again. He drained his mug and reached for his jacket.

"I'll go for the milk," he said. "I'll be passing the cars on the way and I'll stop and top out the snowmobile tank."

I picked up my coat.

"Let's go," I said.

"Stay here," Stan told me. "I can manage alone."

"Not if the snowmobile breaks down," I said.

"I have snowshoes out in the barn. I'll take them along."

I had to get back to the old man's car. He wasn't going there alone, not if I could help it.

"Good idea," I said. "The snowshoes and me. It's no weather for a man to be out in alone."

"I'll be okay. You stay here."

I was going to have to say there was something I needed out of my car. My trouble was that I couldn't think of what it could be. I was wondering whether he would believe a toothbrush.

Sally stepped into it.

"Go with him, Matt," she said. "I worry."

"Nothing to worry about," Stan grumbled.

Sally forced a laugh.

"What difference does that make?" she said. "You know me. I worry about nothing. So what else is new? Matt's going with you."

We went out together and made a detour to the barn for the snowshoes. When we came back out to head for the snowmobile, we were well loaded. We had the empty gas cans. I was carrying my skis and Stan was carrying his snowshoes.

The Kellys had come out. They were all wrapped up in their coats and scarves and she had the suitcase. She was already loaded on to the snowmobile and he was about to jump aboard. Stan shouted at them.

Kelly whirled around. He had a pistol in his hand. I had been right about that. There wasn't enough heft to him for handling a revolver. He was the pistol type.

"Stand back," he said. "We're taking it."

"The hell you are," Stan roared and lunged toward him.

There was too much snow underfoot. There was no good ground for lunging. His feet skidded out from under him and he slammed down flat on his face in the snow. I was right beside him and I heard the bullet whistle past me. If Stan had kept his feet, it would have taken him in the belly or in the chest.

I crouched down beside Stan and held him down. Those Kellys were mean and they were crazy. I didn't know how far I could get reasoning with them, but Kelly had the gun and there was nothing for it but to try. At worst I might win a little time. Sally and Dawson were in the house. It wasn't possible that they hadn't heard the shot.

"Make sense," I said. "The snow has everything covered over. You can't tell road from fields. You'll just get yourselves lost out there and you'll freeze to death before anyone can find you."

"Don't listen to him," Mrs. Kelly said.

"If you're smart, you will listen," I argued. "When you first come out, you don't feel how cold it is. It won't be long before you will feel it. You're committing suicide."

"You can worry about that," Kelly said.

He turned to climb on the snowmobile but he couldn't make it without turning his back on us.

"I'll take the gun," Mrs. Kelly said.

She grabbed it out of his hand. It was obvious that it wasn't the first time she'd held one. Don't ask me what she'd done with those nerves of hers. No nervous woman could have had so steady a hand.

If we had been closer, I could have made a try at taking her, but when someone has a gun on you, everything hangs on distance. Those little pistols are short-range weapons. Unless you're in pretty close they aren't reliably accurate. At close range, however, they'll kill just as dead as any heavier weapon.

If your man with the gun is inexperienced and he's worried enough about being within accurate range, he's likely, as often as not, to ram the thing right into your gut or at least hold it on you close enough for it to be within your reach. When it's like that, you can handle it. All you need is a reasonably quick hand. You can slap it off target. It's a matter of only a split second. Even if he sees you making your move and he moves with you, squeezing off his shot, your hand is going to be just that touch faster than any guy's trigger finger can be. Even if you're not in time to make it miss you completely, you'll be in time at least to turn what would have been a bullet in your heart or in your gut into nothing more than a grazing wound.

I knew all that, but it was doing me no good. The gun was out of reach by about three steps, just near enough for accuracy, nowhere near close enough for me to hope to get a hand on it.

"You'll be dead out there in the snow," I said, "and Firpo will run out of milk. That's something they'll hold against you down in hell. I'd guess they have a special hell for people who take milk away from babies."

While I was jabbering, I was trying to send out thought waves. I had them targeted on Dawson. If he came through the door of the house, he'd be coming up behind them. He could take them easily from the rear while they were holding the gun on us.

The house door opened and Dawson stood framed in the doorway. The stupid lug just stood there with his mouth hanging open, gaping. Shoving him aside, Sally lunged past him. She had a cast-iron skillet in her hand. She wasn't stopping to gape. Swinging the thing like a tennis racket, she caught the Kelly woman on the side of the head with the flat of the skillet. The pistol dropped and la Kelly toppled off the snowmobile and lay twitching slightly in the snow.

Before Kelly even knew what was happening, Sally took another swing. Again she was right on target. She had both of the Kellys decked. I jumped forward and grabbed the pistol.

VI

We dragged them into the house. They were both conscious, but Sally had taken all the fight out of them. She was my idea of the perfect housewife, a great hand with the kitchen utensils. They were putting on an act of heavy damage, but it was obvious that they hadn't been badly hurt. Kelly, in fact, even while we were dragging them in out of the snow, was sufficiently himself to take a firm hold on that suitcase. He brought it along with him.

He wasn't saying a word. His wife did all the talking. Resurrecting her nerves, she threw them at us. She was having palpitations. She couldn't stand it. Her nerves were driving her crazy. If she had to remain another moment cooped up with thieves and murderers, she would go out of her mind. Anything was better than that. They were within their rights. Nobody was ever going to say they weren't. They had the right of self-defense.

"We were going into town," the Kelly woman said. "We were going to the police. They would have come out here and taken the lot of you in. They go after murderers. You can bet on that."

Stan let her go on until she had simmered down. Sally was about to answer the woman but, at a gesture from him, she stepped back and let Stan take over.

"I'm going for the milk," he said. "When I come back, I'll

also have plenty of gas. I'll take you into town then. If you want to get away from here, that's okay. It won't be too soon for us. We'll be glad to be shut of you. For now, though, you're going to stay here and you're not going to give any trouble. I'm making sure of that. Before I go, we're going to search you."

While he was talking, he brought his revolver out. He took the slugs out of his pocket and reloaded. Handing me the gun, he told me to keep Mrs. Kelly covered.

"I'll handle him," he said.

Kelly just stood there and let Stan pat him down. Although Stan did a thorough job of it, he came up with nothing. He reached for the suitcase.

Mrs. Kelly made a move toward him. I cocked the revolver. She heard the click and she dropped back. Kelly grabbed the suitcase with both hands and hung on.

"No," he screamed.

Stan wrenched it away from him. Kelly reached for Stan. He was trying to claw at him. Sally picked up her skillet. Kelly kept screaming.

"No . . . you can't . . . you have no right."

Stan planted the flat of his hand against the man's face and pushed him off. Kelly went down hard on his butt. Sally set the skillet down.

"I'm taking this," Stan said. "I'm taking it upstairs and I'm locking it away where you can't get at it. When I get you to town, I'll return it to you, but you're not going to have it until then. It's that or you can hand me the key and I'll search it. How do I know? You can have all kinds of guns in there."

"That's robbery," Kelly yelled.

"Call it what you like. When I get you to town, you can bring charges."

He walked out with the suitcase and we could hear him go up the stairs.

Sally turned to me.

"Keep him covered, Matt," she said, "while I search her. Shoot him if you have to and I just hope you have to."

"Don't you dare touch me," Irene snarled.

"As you prefer," Sally told her. "I can hold the gun on your husband while Matt feels you up. Maybe you'd like that better."

That did it. The Kelly woman went on about Sally's filthy mouth and Sally's filthy mind, but she held still while Sally patted her down. Sally had watched Stan's performance and she was making hers at least as thorough. She was still at it when Stan came back into the room. He waited till Sally had finished. The woman had nothing on her.

Taking the gun out of my hand, Stan passed it to Dawson.

"You take over, Bert," he said. "Keep them quiet till we get back."

Dawson pushed the revolver back at him.

"I'll go with Matt," he said. "You stay here. You can't leave Sally and Firpo alone with them."

"They won't be alone. You're here. Sally can hold the gun if you won't. She can handle them."

"I don't even need a gun," Sally said.

She looked as though she might be wishing for a chance to work them over some more.

"I can go for the milk and gas," Dawson argued. "Your responsibility is here."

"My responsibility is getting that milk," Stan said.

He started to hand the revolver to Sally. Looking sheepish, Dawson took it from his hand.

"All right," he mumbled. "If you want it that way."

"I want it that way," Stan snapped. He turned to me. "Let's go, Matt."

We pulled out to the snowmobile and now Stan was hurrying. There wasn't time for as much as a word before he had the thing roaring. This time he didn't head off across the fields. He took it out to the road and turned left. I knew we were on the road because we were thundering through an avenue of trees. We would be going back past the two cars, the old man's and Baby. Apart from the trees, one piece of ground under the covering of snow was indistinguishable from the next.

He stopped alongside the old man's car. It was recognizable only as a mound of snow that had something of the shape of a car. Together we dug in far enough to get at the gas tank. While we were digging, we were able to talk.

"You're going to run them into town and just let them loose?" I asked.

Stan shook his head.

"I'll have to take them one at a time," he said. "First one and then the other. I'll take them to the police. They can make their charges and I'll make mine. If nothing else, I caught them trying to steal the snowmobile and they did it at the point of a gun. I can charge them with that and I've got witnesses. Then there's the goddamn suitcase. What about that, Matt? Is it theirs or is it old man Hoffman's?"

"It's initialed MK," I said.

"Yeah? I didn't notice but that don't mean they can't have something of the old man's in it."

"The way they tried to fight you on it," I agreed. "That's something."

Although he had opened up that line of thought himself, now he started to back away from it.

"Of course," he said. "It can be she has her jewelry in it or something like that and if they think one of us ripped off your two hundred and they've got ideas of murder on old man Hoffman, it could be nothing more than they didn't want us seeing her jewelry or whatever."

"Where did you find them, Stan?" I asked. "Where's their car?"

"Around on the other road."

"How would they get here?"

"If they killed the old man and robbed him, they figured they'd drive on and be well away from here before anyone found him. They didn't figure they'd get snowed in."

I could think of several ways in which that was impossible and no way that he could be believing a word of what he was saying. Either he just wasn't thinking or he was thinking too much, and this wasn't the time for trying to find out which.

We got the snow cleared away to the place where he could get at the gas tank, and I left him to siphon the gas. I moved around to the door I'd opened when I first came on the body. The window was coated with snow and ice. Rubbing at it with my glove, I cleared it enough to see into the car. If it was going to be there, I expected it would be lying on the back seat or on the floor in back, but it wasn't. It was there and in the one place where it shouldn't have been. It was on the seat in front, not on the driver's seat but alongside.

I very much wanted to get at it but it was going to involve digging the drifted snow away to free the door. I could hardly manage that without telling Stan what I was after and every thought I had in my head was yelling at me that he was the last guy in the world I should be telling it to. I had built a great liking for the guy. There was nothing I wanted more than to call him a friend and now, with that thing lying there on the car seat, more than ever I couldn't trust him. Try as I would, I couldn't see him as a cold-blooded killer, and yet, if he had done it, it would have been nothing but in cold blood.

I was just standing there gaping—trying to get my thoughts sorted out. It was a dispatch case. It was neat and black with good leather and good brass. I was so fixed on it that Stan had come up beside me before I knew he'd moved. He was with me looking in that car window. I said nothing, waiting for him to speak. Everything could depend on how he handled it.

"Keerist," he said. "You see that thing?"

"I see it."

"It wasn't there when we pulled the body out. When we hauled the body across the seat, the case would have come tumbling out with it. It just couldn't have been there."

"That's what I've been thinking," I said.

I wasn't about to tell him the rest of what I was thinking. The whole thing was fitting together. He kills the old man and steals the dispatch case. He takes it home and stows it away, then he goes out again to pretend that he's discovering the body. He has to wait until night when he can be sure he's alone before he opens the dispatch case and empties it. He needs the old man's keys—I was remembering the little luggage key I had felt on the old guy's key ring. During the night he opens the case and he returns the keys to the old man's pocket. He runs the dispatch case back to the car and stupidly leaves it in the one place where it couldn't possibly have been. It's that trip that brings the gas down almost to the bottom of the tank.

It fitted together, but there were flaws in it. I was wondering whether they were real flaws or just the trouble I was having getting past my liking for the big lug. I was wondering whether all of us could have been sleeping so soundly that we wouldn't have heard him. The roar of the snowmobile would have shaken the house. Now I had cleared the window, and I had been standing there looking at the case. He couldn't for a minute have kidded himself that I wasn't seeing it. It came to him that he'd made a stupid mistake. There would be no way he could cover himself except by pretending that it wasn't his mistake. It was some other guy's. Say a guy like Matthew Erridge.

"We've got to get it out of there," he said.

He started digging at the snow where it was banked against the door.

"Why?" I asked.

"Someone could come along and steal it."

"Like who?"

"Like anybody. Even like the snowplow crew when they finally get in here to open up the road."

I set to work shoveling along with him. It was a crazy feeling, standing with him shoulder to shoulder, sweating it out together and thinking I had all it would take to hang him and being all too sure that he for his part was figuring to get himself clear by framing me. I'd never before had it like that with anyone, this buddy feeling all mixed up with suspicion and distrust.

"How is he for gas?" I asked.

"Nearly nothing," he said. "I'd hardly begun siphoning before it ran dry. That's why I was so quick. All I got was maybe a couple of cupfuls."

"He must have been stuck in there a long time with the engine running," I said.

"Yeah. He didn't have enough left to take him anywhere near his house. He could maybe have made it to my place or Bert's, if that far."

"Poor old guy," I said. "A man gets that old, he has the right to die easy."

"He has the right to die on his own. He has the right not to be murdered," Stan growled.

"We've all got that right," I said.

He sighed and changed the subject.

"You don't believe Sally stepped on the rake," he said. "You think I hung that mouse on her."

"None of my business," I said.

"I as good as did," he said. "I shouldn't have left the rake lying out there and when it started snowing, I should have put it away in the barn even if it was only to keep it from lying out there and rusting. A good rake costs money."

"We all forget things now and then," I said.

"Yeah, and most times it doesn't matter too much, but this time it mattered."

He wanted to talk about it. I wondered what was going on in his head. He had to know that I was thinking he was a murderer. It seemed to be important to him that I not think he was a wifebeater as well.

He kept on with it. The way he told it, he'd been watching the snow come down. First the power lines went and then the telephone. He'd been busy turning the water off and draining the pipes. He'd realized that it was no ordinary snowstorm. The roads were going to be blocked. He'd gone out a couple of times and had walked through the snow to the road. When he saw that nothing was moving on it, he decided that he had to take the snowmobile out and check along the road. There would be people stuck in their cars, and he had the means for bringing them in.

"I couldn't go right off," he said. "I had to build the fire up first and I had to help Sally move the stuff she thought we'd need into that one room we could keep warm. While we were doing that, the road was getting worse and worse and I was getting more and more worried."

He was blaming himself for not having thought then to lay in a good supply of Firpo's milk.

So he went out to look for people stuck in their cars. Sally hadn't wanted him to go, and they had argued about it.

"She was afraid for me," he said. "That's the way she is. She'll never be afraid for herself, but she'll be afraid for me. I guess it is because she knows that she has better sense than me."

She went out after him, trying to stop him. With the snow covering the rake, she stepped on it.

"I was taking off," he said. "I never saw it happen. I guess she screamed, but you know the noise the snowmobile makes. You don't hear anything else. I didn't know it happened till I came back with those damn Kellys. I should have left them to freeze in their car."

We had enough of the snow cleared from the door. He grasped the handle and put all his weight into the pull. The door came open. He reached in and brought out the dispatch case. Stripping off his thick gloves, he tried the locks.

"Putting his fingerprints on it before a witness," I thought.

The case was locked. He couldn't open it.

"We'll take it back with us," he said. "The key's in his pocket."

"And what are we going to prove?" I asked.

"We'll know whether it's full or empty."

"And then what?"

"If it's full, then he wasn't robbed and he wasn't killed. He just had an accident."

"And if it's empty?" I asked.

"Then we'll know. It was murder and robbery."

There was too much wrong with that, but standing around in that freezing air talking about it wasn't going to do either of us any good.

There would be time later to straighten out his thinking for him and meanwhile I might come to some decisions on whether I wanted to set him right. I thought about it while we were moving on down the road to the hump in the snow that was Baby.

Again we had the job of digging down to where we could get at the gas tank. While we dug, I had the thought that it might be well if I had a look inside. If I was being fitted for a frame, something might have been put in there. I'd left Baby locked, but all through the night I'd been separated from my keys. They had been in one of my pants pockets just as the billfold had been.

I stayed with Stan while he was siphoning out the gas it took to top out the snowmobile tank.

"Take the rest of it," I told him, "as much as the cans will hold."

"The full tank will be more than enough to get us to where we can fill the cans," Stan said.

"Take it anyway, just in case we don't find any pumps that are working."

I left him to the siphoning, and I started working at clearing one of Baby's windows so that I could look in.

"You need something out of there?" he asked.

"I need to know whether something I couldn't possibly want has been put in there."

"What?" he asked. "Why?"

"I don't know what. Why? I didn't kill the old man and I didn't rob him, but it looks as though I was closer to him than anyone else when it happened. Of course, I couldn't have been as close as the guy who killed him, but nobody knows about him and you do know about me. I could be framed for this thing all too easily."

"You talk like you know for sure he was murdered and robbed."

"I know for sure," I said.

"How can you know?"

I had Baby's window cleared and I was looking in. I could see nothing. It was possible, of course, that something had been stowed in the glove compartment, but I decided it wasn't likely enough to make worthwhile all the digging it would take to get the door open.

I went back to Stan just as the first can topped out. I handed him the second can. Even out there in the open the smell of gasoline was strong, not as bad as it had been in Dawson's closed garage but enough to sting your eyes. Stan's eyes were red with it. I took over from him on the siphoning.

"It makes no difference," I said, "whether the dispatch case is stuffed with diamonds or as empty as a gambler's heart. It wasn't there when we pulled the body out of the car. Someone had taken it away and, after we were gone, someone came back to the car and put the dispatch case on the seat. He made the mistake of putting it in the one place where it couldn't possibly have been when we were taking the body out of there. There's no getting around that."

"Then it'll be empty," Stan said.

"Not necessarily. That will depend on how greedy the guy is or how cagey. He went back to the car to return the dispatch case. The only reason he could have for doing that would be to make it look as though there had been no robbery. The old man's dead. There's probably no one to know just how many stones he might have had in there."

Stan nodded.

"He could take out one or two big jobs and leave the rest," he said.

"Right. That's if it isn't empty, but empty won't prove anything either."

"It'll prove robbery."

"You can't be sure. If the old man was a dealer, he bought diamonds and he sold diamonds. What's to say he wasn't headed somewhere to make a buy? He carries the empty case to put them in or, taking it the other way around, what's to say he hadn't sold everything he was carrying?"

"So it's maybe robbery and maybe not?" Stan asked.

"On the robbery angle only one thing is sure. It was attempted robbery," I said.

My gas ran out, but Stan was satisfied. He said we had enough to take us into town and back several times over even if we found no pumps working.

"How many days can this snow last?" he said. "It won't go on forever and the plows will be coming through."

"Okay," I said. "If it lasts too long, we can still go around to that other road and tap Kelly's tank."

"Them." Stan took time out to spit. "We can if we have to, but I'd just as soon not touch anything of theirs. He was such a nice old guy."

We took off again and now we were backtracking on the road I'd come before the snow stopped me. We didn't stay with it long. After a short distance Stan turned off onto a feeder road. Driving in that zero visibility, I had missed it. If I had seen it, I could probably have made it all the way into the town before things closed down.

About a hundred yards beyond the turnoff we hit a gas station. The office window was lighted and the man was ready to pump gas. We took enough to top out the second can.

We'd be going back with each of us having a full gas can lashed to his back. We were still going to have the milk to carry and Stan wanted to carry a lot of milk. We went on to the dairy. They had light and everything was working.

We were thinking that the break in the power lines had been at some place beyond the dairy and the gas station, but the dairyman told us that theirs had also been knocked out.

"It only just came back on," he said. "Maybe less than a half hour ago. It's lucky they got it fixed while the weather is still this cold. Even while it was out we were okay without refrigeration."

Stan crossed his fingers.

"I hope mine is back on," he said.

The dairyman was a gloomy type. He seemed to enjoy dashing Stan's hope.

"I hear tell," he said, "there was more than one break. It'll be a time before they get them all fixed. This is the worst there's ever been. All the way back to where they weren't keeping no records, there's never been one this bad. Never this much snow and never this cold."

"You're telling me?" Stan said.

"All up and down the roads they been pulling people half frozen out of their cars," the dairyman said. "They got a couple even that didn't make it, a couple of dead ones."

The guy had a taste for catastrophe. He was brimming with bad news and he'd been having too few opportunities to unload it.

"I know," Stan told him. "We've got people back at our place and one, he was dead before I got to him."

"Yeah? Anybody we know?"

"Mr. Hoffman. He was the old man had a house out the north fork, came to it summers and like weekends."

"Hoffman?" the dairyman repeated the name. "No. I don't know him."

"He was such a nice old guy," Stan said. "Everybody liked him. It's a terrible thing."

"Yeah. If it wasn't for them snowmobiles, there'd be a lot more dead."

"I guess everybody who has one has been out doing what he can," Stan said.

I was saying nothing but I was asking myself if that mightn't have been for me. He could have been making the point that Stan Sobieski hadn't been the only man out ranging the roads on his snowmobile.

Going back to the house, I had my hands full hanging onto the milk. Back on the main road we kept passing lights that shone through the falling snow. These were the lights I had been looking for. The windows had been there all the time but the power failure had blacked them out.

When we came off the road at the Sobieski place, the lights there were shining through the snow. I looked at Stan. He had his scarf covering his whole face up to his eyes, but his eyes showed it. He had to be grinning from ear to ear. Sally came out to meet us. She'd been waiting till she saw the milk I was carrying before she was going to let herself be happy. She saw it and the joy came up in her.

"We have lights," she said. "The furnace has started up. Everything else is going. As soon as you get the water turned back on, we'll have that too."

"Right away," Stan told her. "As soon as we've stowed the gasoline in the barn. I don't want to take it into the house."

She brought the milk into the house while Stan and I carried our gas cans into the barn. He was also carrying the dispatch case. This time he was the one who went into the old man's pockets. He brought out the keys and he fitted the little one to the locks on the dispatch case. They opened and he threw back the lid.

The case was empty.

He stood over it looking at it and he sighed.

"Like you said, it doesn't prove anything."

"Murder and robbery or murder and attempted robbery," I told him.

"Attempted robbery, yes, Matt. What makes you so sure of murder? It could be the old man had an accident and it was just robbing the dead."

"He had an accident and then I had the same kind of accident," I said. "Old people have accidents like that. I'm not nearly that old, Stan, not yet."

"Why you? For two hundred bucks?"

"It's been done," I said. "You see it in the papers all the time. Guys have been killed for a lot less."

"Kelly?"

"Maybe, but then only if the old man died by accident and somebody robbed him or attempted to after he was dead. Then it could be that Kelly got ideas and tried it on me. Any other way, it's too much. Nobody can believe it. One guy kills the old man and another guy tries to do an imitation of it. It's possible, but it's too unlikely."

"Those Kellys, they're no good. We know that."

"Yes. We know that, but there's no way he could have gotten back and forth to the old man's car all those times. She ripped off my two hundred, but sneak thieves are one thing; murder's something else."

"Shooting at me. That was the same something else. It would have been murder."

"There's still the impossibility. You say they came on the old man. He's in his car, stuck in the snow. They kill him and grab off the dispatch case and then they go rolling on to where you found them. How do they roll when he was stuck? He wasn't having his own private little blizzard and the road clear for everyone else. And that's only the beginning. You have to get one of them back to the car after we took the body out, back there to return the dispatch case and then all the way back to the house. I'd like to think it was the Kellys. I can't think of another couple who'd be better suited to it, but everything we know says it can't be."

"Then you're thinking me," Stan said.

"Just as you're thinking me and me out to frame you," I said. "It could be you, Stan, and you out to frame somebody. First it was me you had picked for it and then, when the Kellys got to looking bad, you shifted to thinking you'd have a better chance if you switched to sticking it on them."

"Yes," he said. "Except that all along it's been hard to believe and only because you're my kind of a guy. We could be buddies."

"Exactly," I said. "All along I've been having the same trouble with it."

He grinned at me.

"What does that make us, Matt? A pair of murdering crooks?"

I had to grin back at him.

"I suppose that could be a bond between two guys," I said.

VII

We went back to the house. We were both half frozen. The last bit of warmth we'd had was when we'd been inside the dairy and that hadn't been much. The only place in the plant that had been warmed at all was the office and we'd been in there only a few minutes. It hadn't been nearly long enough for taking the chill off us. The office, moreover, hadn't been warm enough to take much of the chill off any-one—the power had only just come on.

Back in the house it was still the old togetherness. The heat was starting to come up but it was the way it had been in the office back at the dairy. There was still only the one warm room. It was going to be a while before the cold would be pushed out of the rest of the house.

With the light showing through the windows the house looked so cozy and cheerful that I suppose I made the mistake of thinking that even the Kellys would have come around to feeling better about things. I knew how I was feeling. The country was coming back to life. Things were beginning to move. Okay. We still would have some waiting to do, but things were going to be a lot easier while we waited.

The Kellys were at one side of the fireplace. Firpo in his crib was at the other side. Dawson was sitting alongside the crib. He had the revolver and he wasn't taking his eyes off the

Kellys. Sally was busy pulling the sheets off all those mattresses she had lying on the floor.

"We'll get the mattresses back," she said, "and we'll sleep in decent beds tonight."

I moved in to give her a hand.

"Last night wasn't bad," I said. "I've had worse nights." I turned to the Kellys. "We were damned lucky Sally and Stan took us in. We couldn't have done better and we could have done a lot worse."

What the hell. We weren't through with each other yet. A man could try to keep it civilized while we were waiting.

The Kellys said nothing; they just sneered at me. They weren't going to play. It wasn't breaking my heart.

Stan planted himself before the fire for a couple of moments. He had the dispatch case dangling from his hand. I knew what he was after. He was looking for a reaction from the Kellys. He wasn't getting any. Only Sally took any notice of it.

"What's that?" she asked. "Where did you get it?"

"Out of Mr. Hoffman's car," Stan told her. "I thought it was better not to leave it there. Somebody might come by and swipe it."

Sally reached for it.

"Let me have it," she said.

Stan wasn't letting it go.

"What'll you do with it?" he asked.

"Take it upstairs and lock it away where it'll be safe," she said. "This isn't the time to be leaving anything valuable lying around loose in here."

If her words didn't carry the message, the look she tossed in the direction of the Kellys couldn't miss.

Irene Kelly spoke to her husband.

"Did you hear that?" she said. "As though there was anything in this dump anybody would want."

"You never know what some people will want," Sally said, "or what they'll take."

"I'll go upstairs with it," Stan said.

Sally shook her head.

"You'll stay here by the fire till you're good and warm," she told him, "and then you'll go and turn the water back on. I'm a woman who likes to be pampered. I'm a demanding wife. I want all sorts of lovely things like johns that'll flush again."

I caught myself wishing the two of them would say or do something that could make me quit liking them. He was my kind of guy and that made it rough. She was my kind of girl and that was making it a lot rougher. Not to speak of Firpo. I looked at him where he was lying in his crib doing an exploration of his toes. He was my kind of baby.

At that point the Kellys started yelling. Stan was going to get them out of there. He had promised them that. They weren't going to stay in the house another minute. They were being held against their will. It was the same as kidnaping. He wasn't going to get away with it. He was going to pay for it. He would see. They were going to make him pay for it if it was the last thing they did.

He stayed by the fire and let them rant. He had his back turned to them and he was acting as though they weren't there, or at least as though he was deaf to their caterwauling. Sally came back into the room. She had disposed of the dispatch case; now she was ready to take on the Kellys.

"Oh, shut up," she said. "If you want to know, I wouldn't at all mind shutting you up. I've had more than enough of you. But you're not the most important thing around here. Actually you're the least important thing. You'll be taken into town when we're ready and no sooner. I've had a mind to lock you away in one of the rooms upstairs where we won't have to look at you and listen to you, but I've been waiting till they warm up. I've wanted you to be comfortable. I'm that kind of a fool, but you bother me and I won't wait. I can lock you up in a cold room. So just shut up and think about that."

I can't say that she silenced them completely. There was never anything that could do that for Irene Kelly, but Sally's threat worked well enough. The complaints, the imprecations, the talk about her nerves, and the promises of retribution went on but they simmered down to a barely audible mumble. It was easy enough to ignore that. Talking among ourselves, we could even wipe out hearing it.

"We can start carrying the mattresses upstairs," Sally said. "We'll get them back on the beds."

Stan and I moved to do it, but she turned us away. She was giving orders. Stan was to remain by the fire and do nothing but warm himself. Once he had the chill off him, he was going to have to get the water turned on and then he would be going out into the cold again.

"We do want to get them out of our hair," she said, indicating the Kellys.

I was also to stay by the fire since I had been out in the cold.

She turned to Dawson.

"Give Matt the gun, Bert," she said. "He can keep an eye on them. You haven't been outside. You're good and warm. You don't have to hug the fire."

"Yes, ma'am," Dawson said, suddenly coming up out of his lethargy and even coming all the way. "I can wrestle the mattresses upstairs by myself. You stay down here where it's warm."

She handed him one of those men-are-so-stupid looks.

"And you'll drag them up the stairs, wiping each step as you go. You'll get them dirty," she said.

It was the housewife speaking. When they began taking up the mattresses, I saw that she had put down a neat layer of clean paper under each of them. She had been forced to improvise but her improvisations had been housewifely. After she and Dawson had taken up the last of the mattresses, they remained upstairs. I guessed that she had him helping her make up the beds. Stan pulled away from the fire and went off to get the water turned on. I was left alone with the Kellys. She opened it up.

"He was into your pockets. He went all through your stuff." She wasn't calling him by name but obviously she was talking about Stan Sobieski. "I never wanted to come here, but what could we do? I knew it was going to be awful. Polacks! You can never trust a Polack. They're animals. You believe all that they're putting out about her eye? Everybody knows Polacks are free with their hands, not that she's any better. He took your money. You know that, don't you?"

"If he did, it's okay," I said. "I owed it to him."

"Then you know he took it."

"All I know is what I saw."

"You saw him in your pockets."

"I saw your husband take a shot at him. I saw you all set to shoot me. I saw her save me from it."

Kelly spoke up.

"It was only a warning shot," he said. "You saw it. I shot into the air. I shot over his head."

That was going to be their story. They were thinking they could suck me into backing them up on it.

"You shot into the air," I said, "but you aimed at his gut.

You shot into the air because he slipped and went down just as you got your shot off. If his footing had been any good, you'd be up for a murder rap. So don't look for any help from me."

"From you?" she screamed. "We don't need any help from you or anyone else. You'll see."

She was off again and there wasn't a chance it would be anything I hadn't heard before. If there was a new note, it was only that we were Americans, the Kellys and I, and we ought to be standing together against "them Polacks."

I knew that if she went on with that Polack line, I was going to have a hard time not slugging her. I didn't want to hear it and I didn't have to. There was the television. Now that we had the power back on, I could bring in the pet-food commercials. If I had to be stuck listening to a cat, I would take Morris, and given a choice of bitches, I could be happier with one who ate Alpo.

I flipped the TV switch. Picture and sound came in. I hit a newscast and, as was to be expected, they were talking about the weather. Buffalo was a disaster area. The whole of the snow belt was paralyzed. The weather prediction was discouraging. Although the snow had slackened off, there was more coming. It was going to be heavy again before it was over and they were making no predictions on how soon it might be over.

This news hit the Kellys hard. The weather report made it obvious that Stan would take them into town and that would be it. They would be stuck there until the weather cleared. I couldn't see where the weather was going to make any big difference to them. They were going to be stuck in any case until they'd answered to the snowmobile-hijacking and attempted-murder charges he was going to bring against them.

How they could have been thinking anything else I couldn't see. They didn't know, of course, that Stan was also kicking around the possibility of accusing them of the Hoffman murder and robbery. Even though there wasn't a chance that the hard evidence wouldn't clear them of that one, the odds were great that the roads would be cleared long before those two could be.

Considering the spot they were in, it seemed strange that the prediction of more snow should be hitting them so hard. They were stuck in any case and, idiotic as I knew them to be, it still seemed impossible that they shouldn't know that it would be a lot more than the snow and the cold that was going to keep them pinned down.

The newscast broke and, sure enough, Morris came on to be seduced by a can of liver-flavored who-knows-what. Then we had some armpits and that twenty-year-old chick who holds off senility by taking her Geritol every day. After the wet paper towel had sustained the weight of two brimming coffee cups, the news came back on with me wondering whether, the next time I got a bridge job, they would want me to build it out of wet paper towels.

The newscast was finished with the weather and on to more run-of-the-mill crime. Two women had been raped and killed in the Bronx. There had been a bank heist in Brooklyn and a murder in Philadelphia. It seemed to be a bad day for banks. There was one in Poughkeepsie that had come up short of some three hundred thousand in bearer bonds and of one branch manager. That item brought the newsboys back to the weather. Absconding bank managers can be hard to find under any conditions, but it's tougher when you've lost one in the snow. The missing manager was a guy named Melvin King. He'd been with the bank twenty-two years.

They were watching the screen. I was watching them. I was thinking of their precious suitcase stowed upstairs. I was remembering the M.K. monogram.

M.K.

Michael Kelly?

Melvin King?

Irene's jewelry?

The Poughkeepsie bank's bearer bonds?

I took a flyer.

"It's going to be one helluva long wait before anybody's going to be able to make it to Canada," I said. "It's snowed in solid from here to the border and beyond."

Irene said nothing. She was back to the old act, distancing herself from the scum. King Kelly took it up.

"That where you were headed?" he asked. "Canada?"

He was making it sound as though he couldn't have cared less. He was just going along on idle conversation to pass the time.

"I was going skiing," I told him. "What were you after? Snowballs?"

"We were down in Florida. We were headed for home. We came back north too soon."

If they'd been in Florida, they'd never been out except at night. White, winter skin, no sun had touched it even briefly.

"Where's home?" I asked.

"What's it to you?"

He'd had enough of the idle conversation.

"Nothing, Mel," I said. "Nothing at all."

I switched the TV off before I said it. I wanted to be sure he heard the name I was putting on him. He gave no sign of hearing it and, if his little woman was looking at me balefully, that represented no change. I couldn't remember when it had last been that she'd had anything for any of us except those same baleful looks.

Stan came back into the room. He was looking well pleased with himself.

"There's one thing I did right," he said. "I got the water turned off and I drained the pipes. I did it the minute the power went. We're okay. Water's back on and I've checked all through the house. We didn't bust a pipe anywhere. No leaks." He turned to his departing guests. "The time's come," he said. "Which do I take first?"

"We'll go together."

That was Irene, if such was her name.

"It's only a snowmobile, lady," Stan told her. "It won't carry more than two. Since one of them's got to be me, figure it out for yourself."

The man of the family took over.

"Look, Sobieski," he said. "We were hasty. We're sorry."

His wife turned that look of hers on him. Whether she was about to slap him in the mouth or just ask him if he'd gone out of his mind I'll never know. He went on talking past her look. She got the message. She even made a try at looking pleasant. For my money she was asking too much of herself.

Meanwhile her husband was giving it the big pitch. He was down and he was crawling. It was cold outside, and neither of them was feeling at all well. Taking a hit in the head from a big, heavy hunk of cast iron leaves a person feeling queasy. They were neither of them in shape to take the cold and the snow.

They weren't blaming anyone. Mrs. Sobieski had been absolutely right in what she did.

"She had to do it," he said. "We weren't ourselves. We'd

just gone out of our minds. She did the right thing, but I can't begin to tell you how sick we're feeling."

He was piling it on. I could see him come down with the thought that he might be giving it too much. Stopping short, he backed off from it a little.

"We'll be all right," he said. "It's not like we need a doctor or anything like that. It's just if we could stay here with you and not go out in the cold while we're feeling so shaky."

I could get a better ring of truth out of a lead quarter. It was obvious that Stan wasn't finding it any more convincing, but I could see he was wavering. I knew what was getting to him. It's a sickening thing to see a man crawl. It's the more sickening if he's crawling to you and you know that you can, if you will, shut it off. You don't have to believe him or even pity him. It can take no more than disgust to break you down.

"I don't know," he mumbled. "I'll have to talk to Sally."

He escaped and went upstairs. King Kelly switched from the phony hangdog look to a smirk. The smirk looked genuine. That made it no easier to take.

"Forget it," his wife snapped. "She won't, not that bitch."

I could have clapped my hands over my ears, but it wasn't the time for clowning.

Stan came back into the room and Sally came with him. She'd brought their suitcase down with her. She was taking charge and, from the set of her chin, I knew that she would be taking no nonsense.

"It's a quick ride and no stops," she said. "I have plenty of warm blankets. You can wrap up in them and be as warm as you like for the ride in."

"But Mrs. Sobieski . . ." Kelly began.

She cut him right off. She wasn't going to listen.

"You're going," she said. "Stan's ready to take you and he's taking you right now. There's plenty else to be done. So get moving."

"I told you," Irene snarled.

Sally ignored it. She turned to Stan.

"Your army blankets," she said. "Take them. I've put the others on the beds."

Stan started out of the room. I handed Sally the revolver and went out after him. I caught up with him on the stairs.

"There's something you've got to know," I said.

"What I know," Stan said, "is how great it's going to be when I've seen the last of those two."

"Right," I said, and I went on to tell him about the missing bank manager.

"M.K.," he said. "Michael Kelly or Melvin King."

"It may not be," I said, "but I'm laying no bets that it isn't."

"It's got to be," Stan said. "It'll be why he's changed his tune. Now that he knows the word is out on him, he doesn't want to go into town. Put that with the way they hang onto that suitcase."

We went on up the stairs to pick up the blankets. Dawson was up there making a bed. I could have told him that he wasn't performing up to any housewife's standards, much less Sally Sobieski's. I could just see her pulling it apart and making it up neatly.

Stan picked up a couple of army blankets that lay folded on a chair. When he started back downstairs with them, I was about to follow him. Dawson dropped a hand on my arm.

"How's about helping me with the bed making?" he said.

It was a reasonable suggestion. I could do a better job of it. I've had army training and it seemed right that I should be pulling part of the load. I stayed with him and we worked on the bed, but only till Stan had trotted down the stairs and was out of earshot.

Dawson dropped the bed making.

"Screw it," he said. "I wanted to talk to you alone."

"What about?"

"Sally and Stan," he said. "They've been great and they won't say it, but they've been stuck with a houseful of people long enough. It's time they had the place to themselves."

"I won't fight that," I said.

"If you look around up here," he continued, "you can see plenty of rooms and plenty of beds, but there's only the one double. You stay here and Stan isn't going to let you be alone for the night. He's going to want you where he can watch you like last night. That'll mean Sally sleeps alone."

"I see what you mean," I said, "but it's going to have to be his choice. He's taking the Kellys in and handing them over to the cops. He can make a third trip and do the same with me. It's going to be up to him, isn't it?"

"It doesn't have to be," Dawson said. "With the power back on, I'll be going home to my place and you can come with me. That way Sally and Stan can have their house to themselves and, what the hell, I can use some help getting stuff going in my place again."

"And you'll take over as my keeper?" I said.

He whacked me on the back and he laughed.

"That's a crock, Matt," he said. "Nobody really believes it. It's only that Stan's a worrier. If he really believed it, he'd be taking you into town to hand you over to the cops too. So while he's making up his mind, I can just tell him I'll keep an eye on you."

From the sound of it, all hell was breaking loose downstairs. It had been going on for some time, but it had now moved out to the downstairs hall and we could hear it.

"The Sobieskis need help," I said.

"Yeah."

Dawson started for the stairs. I went with him. Stan was frogmarching a cursing and struggling King Kelly toward the front door and Sally was holding a screaming Irene at bay. Dawson stepped into it.

"How are you going to handle him on the run into town?" he asked. "He gets to acting up and first thing you know you'll be running the two of you into a tree."

"He gives me any trouble," Stan said, "I'll clip him one. I won't mind. I owe him."

"Why don't we tie him up?" Dawson suggested.

Hearing that, Kelly found some strength he hadn't known he had. He kicked and squirmed. He almost broke away from Stan's grip.

"You do it, Bert," Sally said. "You'll find clothesline out in the laundry room. You can use that."

Stan didn't like it. He made a stab at reasoning with his spitting, squirming, kicking handful.

"Look," he said. "We don't want to tie you up. You going to make us do it?"

Back when I was a kid I had a dog. It was a big one, a Lab. I used to wrestle around with it and sometimes, when I got too rough, it would grab my hand in its teeth. It never bit me. It was just like a threat. When it did that, I wouldn't pull my hand away. I'd leave it in the Lab's mouth and move with him, keeping my hand between his teeth. The dog would get the funniest look. He was embarrassed, stuck with a situation he hated.

Stan was wearing that look. He was embarrassed by his

strength and his size—he didn't want to use them and he was forced into a situation where he didn't know how to get out of it.

Dawson came trotting back with the length of clothesline. He wasn't embarrassed. He lashed a piece of the line around Kelly's ankles and used another piece to tie the man's hands down to his sides. Kelly was trying to fight it, but it was Stan who kept telling Dawson that he was drawing the rope too tight. It did look as though Dawson was a shade too happy about his work. He seemed disposed to turn a precaution into a punishment.

But I said nothing. Stan was carrying the ball. Even though it was colder than it had ever been within living memory, Stan knew these winters well enough to have a good idea of the dangers. Tight bindings aren't healthy under any conditions. In extreme cold they can be an invitation to gangrene. At Stan's insistence Dawson eased up a little on the rope. He still had the guy trussed up good and tight, but it was a little more humane.

Stan slung the guy over his shoulder, carried him outside, and set him down on the snowmobile. Kelly or King, whichever he was, evidently knew a lost cause when he saw one. He had shut up. He looked wild and miserable but he wasn't thrashing around any more and he was saying nothing. Not so Irene. Nothing short of a gag and a strait jacket was ever going to keep that babe quiet. Sally was holding her off, but she could do no more than that.

We saw Stan and his burden on their way and hauled back into the house. By this time the furnace was making itself felt. The hall was pleasantly warm. The room where we'd been doing all our living was an inferno, and Firpo was beginning to look like a boiled baby. Sally moved him out to the kitchen and we went out there with her. It was okay for temperature but in every other way it was hell. Irene had launched into a nonstop tantrum and inevitably her yelling and carrying on set Firpo off. The crying baby didn't stop her any; she just worked at outyelling him.

Sally couldn't take it.

"Enough," she yelled. "I've got nerves too."

She grabbed the King woman—I was well past thinking of them as Kelly—and dragged her out to the hall. It was a battle all the way but somehow she got her up the stairs and locked her in one of the bedrooms. Sally was crying when she came back down. I had picked Firpo up and I was trying to interest him in the one talent I have that I thought might appeal to him. I wiggled my ears till my scalp felt as though it were nothing more than a slip-cover to my skull.

Sally took him from me. She did nothing but hold him in her arms, but he simmered down.

It wasn't all peace, of course. Sally's prisoner upstairs was stamping on the floor and banging on the locked door and yelling her head off. At that distance, with the closed doors between, the yelling came through but keyed down enough so that it was having no effect on Firpo. The stamping and the banging were much louder, but I guess those were noises that didn't bother the kid. They bothered Sally, though.

"Damn that woman," she sobbed. "I hate her. I hate her like I never thought I could hate anybody. I hate her for what she made me do to her. Locking her up like a wild animal, I'm going to have that in nightmares the rest of my born days."

"There are wild animals that don't go on four feet," I said.

"I suppose," Sally said, "but I've never had to know them."

Stan was gone for well over an hour and Sally took to worrying. He was going only as far as the police barracks and that was a good piece this side of the town. He should have been there and back several times over. She was thinking the snowmobile had broken down and he was stuck somewhere, or that, even trussed up as he was, Stan's prisoner had thrashed around and run them into an accident.

She hit the phone and tried to get through to the barracks, but she could get nothing but busy signals. She went outside to look, as though just by looking she could bring him home. She'd stay out until the cold had bitten into her and then she'd come back in, only to go out again even before she was properly warmed up.

It came to be time for Firpo's bottle and she fixed it for him. She worked at pushing off her fears.

"He'll have to eat when he gets here," she said. "It's long past time for lunch. I'm not going to let him go out again until I've given him a hot meal."

She made herself busy, scurrying from refrigerator to freezer to stove. The big skillet she had used for taming the royal pair went on the stove. She browned a mess of pork chops in it. She loaded a big kettle with sauerkraut, tossed in a jar of canned tomatoes, added peppercorns, juniper berries, and I don't know what all else and set that to simmer. She added a lot of Polish sausage to the skillet to brown with the chops.

She dashed away from that to make corn bread and she left her bread mixing to add the browned chops and sausage to the kettle. Leaving those to simmer, she poured the corn bread batter into three pans and shoved them into the oven.

She was back at the telephone collecting busy signals when we heard the snowmobile. The din from upstairs had first diminished and then simmered down to nothing. I could guess that Irene had banged her hands bloody and worn out her heels, but the roar of the snowmobile brought her back to life. The stamping and banging and screaming started up again.

Sally disregarded it. She dropped the phone and in her hurry she didn't even stop to set it back on the hook. We followed after her. On my way past I hung the phone up for her.

We caught up with them as they were coming into the house. Stan was worrying about her because she had run out without so much as stopping to fling a sweater over her shoulders.

He looked haggard. I've seen men when they've first come out of battle and firemen when they are carrying charred bodies out of a burning house. He had that look. It was the look of a man who had just been face to face with hell and was carrying it in his eyes.

She was asking him what had kept him so long. Was he all right? What had happened?

"Nothing," he said. "I was held up all this time over at the barracks. It's them. His driver's license, credit cards, Social Security card, all that stuff—Melvin King."

"And the bearer bonds in the suitcase?" I asked.

"It figures," Stan said. "They won't know for sure till I bring her in. They couldn't open the suitcase. No key. It figures she's got the key."

"You're not going anywhere until you've eaten," Sally said.

"I told them I'd bring her in."

"They can wait. They can play with their telephone until you get her there."

"God," Stan said, "it's crazy over there. Everybody's got an emergency. One guy called in. He's desperate—cooped up in the house without any TV, he and his wife and the kids, they'll go crazy. He wants them to get a new tube out to him right away. Some folks have real troubles."

Sally tore off for the kitchen. She was remembering her corn bread.

Stan stood for a moment, listening to the thunder from above.

"What's she doing up there?" he asked.

"Sally took her up and locked her in," Dawson told him.

"She'll be tearing the bedroom apart," Stan said.

"Down here she was tearing Firpo apart," I explained. "Her yelling was scaring the kid and that got him to yelling. Sally couldn't take it. Another woman would have killed her."

VIII

Sally called us out to the kitchen. She had the bread out of the oven and she was dishing up her hunter's stew. The Michelin guys should have been there, or maybe not. They don't have but three stars, never enough for rating Sally Sobieski. She was heaping up five plates.

"Do I bring her down to eat?" Stan asked.

"Over my dead body," Sally told him. "If Firpo has to take any more of her yelling, he's going to grow up nervous."

Stan reached for one of the plates.

"I'll take it up to her," he said.

"No," Sally said. "You've had more than enough of those two and you're not through yet, God help you. I'll go up."

Dawson brushed past her and took the plate out of Stan's hand.

"I'll go," he said. "She doesn't bother me any."

Stan watched him out of the kitchen. He sighed.

"I wish I was like him," he said. "Like him or like the cops. I guess you've got to be made for it if you're going to be a cop. I know I'm doing the right thing. There was nothing else I could do, but still I wish it could have been some other guy had to do it. I wish it didn't have to be me."

"Eat your food while it's still hot," Sally said.

We ate. Nobody needed to be told. A guy would have to

be blind and without a nose if he was going to hold back from tucking into it.

Dawson was a long time coming back down. Sally began worrying about him. His food was going to be cold. She got up and set his plate in the oven to keep it hot, but she fretted.

"What's he doing up there?" she said. "Holding her on his lap and feeding it to her?"

We had almost finished by the time Dawson came down. He was looking sheepish and he was carrying the pieces of a broken plate in his hands with the chop and the sausage and the cabbage piled up on the broken pieces of crockery.

"She took it from me and threw it in my face," he said. "I been cleaning it up off the floor and washing it out of my hair and my shirt and pants. I used one of your towels, Sally. It's up in the bathroom all soaking wet and stained with the stuff."

His shirt and pants were wet and there was water dripping out of his hair.

"Never mind the towel," Sally said. "It'll go in the washer. Did she burn you?"

"Not to notice," he said. "Just messed me up."

His face was red but not more than always. There didn't seem to be any scald marks.

"Then sit down. I've been keeping yours hot for you."

She took his plate out of the oven and set it down before him, warning him not to touch the hot plate.

"What are we going to do about her eating?" Stan asked.

"I'll tell you what we're going to do, Mr. Stanley Sobieski, you beautiful dope," Sally said. "We're going to let her go hungry. For all I care, she can starve till she gets to the police barracks and they give her the peacock tongues or whatever it is her ladyship fancies."

"I'm sorry about the plate," Dawson said.

"Never mind," Sally said. "It wasn't a good plate and anyhow it's my fault. I should have sent it up to her in a dog dish. I'm going to have the plate stuffed and keep it on the mantelpiece to remember her by."

"I want to get her out of here so we can forget her," Stan said, "her and him, like we never saw them."

Sally sighed.

"I wish you didn't have to take her in. Couldn't somebody from the barracks come out for her? It's their job, not yours. They've got snowmobiles, haven't they?"

"They've been running all over the place night and day," Stan said. "Diabetics running out of their insulin, people they have to get to the hospital because it's their time to be on the kidney machine. Till you get a thing like this, you never know how many people there are, you see them around and they look healthy, but it's only from day to day because it's the insulin or the kidney machine or like that it's keeping them alive."

"So you volunteer to do their work for them."

"Yeah, I volunteered to help them out, Sally, but I'm not kidding myself. It was more for us than for them. It's taking her in or it's keeping her here till they can get around to coming out here for her."

Sally moaned. "Then you'll have to take her," she said. "If we have to keep her around waiting for them, I'll kill her. I came close. I don't trust myself."

Stan drank down the last of his coffee.

"I'll get her out of here," he said, pushing away from the table. "You stay away from it, Sally. You've had more than enough."

"And you haven't?" Sally asked him.

"I'll do what I've got to do and we'll be through with it," he said.

"Come back as quick as you can."

"I will, but don't worry if I'm a while. I can be stuck at the barracks again. I tried to call you, but I couldn't get to the phone when it wasn't in use."

"I won't worry," she promised, "now that I know what it is."

"You shouldn't have worried before," he said. "You know I can take care of myself."

"You remember to do just that. Firpo needs a father and I need a husband. There was a time before we were married when I was fine sleeping alone. Now that I've tried it again, I know that I don't like it."

Stan grinned and blushed. He pulled her up against him and buried his face in her neck to kiss her.

Dawson caught my eye and nodded. He was reminding me of what he'd been saying upstairs.

They broke out of it. Sally stayed in the kitchen with Firpo and started clearing away after the meal. Dawson, Stan, and I went upstairs to get Mrs. King down to the snowmobile. By the door to the room Sally had locked her in there was a wet spot on the hall floor. That was where Dawson had cleaned up.

Stan unlocked the door. We were expecting her to come out fighting, but we found her a changed woman. She was ready to go along. More than that, she was eager to go. It couldn't be too quick for her. She wanted to be out of that horrible house and never see it again. She wanted to be with her Michael.

"His name is Melvin," Dawson said. "Didn't you know?"

"That's a lie," she said.

Going down the stairs, she grumbled about having been locked up. She complained about having been kept without food.

"It's your own fault," Dawson said. "I brought it to you."

"You brought what to me?"

It sounded as though she might be telling us that the hunter's stew and the corn bread had been unfit to eat.

"The same as we had," Dawson said, "and it was good. If you were hungry, you wouldn't have thrown it in my face."

"Thrown it in your face?" she said. "That's a lie. I never threw anything in your face. Nobody brought me anything. I never saw your ugly face."

Dawson shrugged. Nobody bothered to argue it. The evidence was there in that wet spot on the floor of the upstairs hall. She wasn't putting up a fight and nobody was caring much about what she was saying.

Downstairs, while she was getting into her coat and wrapping her scarf around her head, Dawson asked Stan if he'd brought the clothesline back with him.

"I brought it back," Stan said, "but leave it. We don't need it."

I suppose it was partly machismo and partly that he was fooled by the docile and even eager way she was getting ready to go with him. More than that, he wanted to think there was no need for tying her up.

"If it was me," Dawson said, "I wouldn't trust her."

"So it isn't you, Bert," Stan snapped.

It was a thing he didn't want to talk about. He wanted to do what he had to do and have it over with.

Dawson caught the signals. He dropped it. Changing the subject, he asked if Stan could take one of the gasoline cans in with him and get it filled.

"I'll need it for my snowmobile," he said.

"Sure thing," Stan said, and started to the barn to pick up one of the empty cans.

The King woman erupted into fresh complaints. People were making every excuse they could think of for holding her against her will. She was being kept waiting out in the cold. She'd never been treated like that in all her life. Nobody had any consideration.

She wasn't held up for long. Stan was back with the empty in almost no time at all. They took off and we went back into the house.

"You heard what Sally said about sleeping alone," Dawson began.

"Yes, I heard her. The problem is can you cook the way she does?"

"I have steaks in the freezer. I'll fry us steaks."

"I like mine broiled and rare," I said.

"You can take yours off before it's cooked."

"It's a deal," I said, "if we can sell Stan."

"I'll sell him," Dawson said. "He wants to be sold."

I went through to the kitchen, thinking I'd help Sally with the dishes. Dawson stayed in the room with the TV. He switched it on and came in on the middle of an old Doris Day movie. It was all right in there. The fire was out and the last glow had gone out of the ashes. The room had cooled down to a livable temperature.

Sally was well along with the cleaning up.

"Let me do the dishes," I said.

"Nothing to do. I have them rinsed off. I'll just put them in the dishwasher."

I'd forgotten about dishwashers.

"Go out and watch TV," she said. "I'll be out in a minute."

"I don't like TV," I said. "And daytime TV is the worst kind."

"I've been thinking about poor Mr. Hoffman out there in the barn," she said. "It doesn't seem right. I didn't want him out there at all, but that horrible woman . . . and now that I'd like to bring him into the house and I could since we're rid of her, I suppose it'd be the wrong thing with the heat on."

"One of the rooms you're not using," I suggested. "We could turn the heat off in the one room if it would make you feel better about him."

She gave me one of those smiles. It was like when I set the grill up for her to heat Firpo's bottle or when I came up with the idea of siphoning the gas out of the cars so we could go and get a fresh supply of milk. I was Erridge, the problem solver. It wasn't enough to make her look at me the way she looked at Stan, but that would have been too much to expect. What she was handing me was good.

"We could do that, couldn't we?" she said.

She turned on the dishwasher and started out. Going through a door that led directly from the kitchen to the hall, she crossed the hall and opened the door to a room on the other side of the house. It was cold in there, as cold as any of the house had ever been. It was a fancier room than any of the others. There had been a time when it would have been called the parlor and would have been rarely used. I didn't know what she would call it, but it had the parlor look. It hadn't been lived in much.

She gave a little laugh.

"I am a fool," she said. "I just didn't think. We never keep the heat on in here because of the furniture."

There was a long table in the middle of the room. It had a

bowl on it and a couple of porcelain birds. She moved them to a smaller table.

"We can put him here," she said.

"Like me to bring him in?" I asked.

"Would you?"

"Why not?" I said.

I went out to the barn, thinking it would be no problem except for the fact that for the first time in all this I was feeling guilty about what I was about to do. I was thinking of what Stan would make of it if he knew. Before I picked up the body, I went through the pockets again. This time I checked the old man's billfold. Unlike mine, it hadn't been stripped. I found thirty-odd dollars and a flock of credit cards. In another pocket I found a checkbook. It was inconclusive, since I had no way of knowing whether the old man had been in the habit of carrying little cash or much. A smart crook could have taken hundreds and left this token of thirty-odd to make it look as though there had been no robbery. On the other hand, a man who went well armed with credit and who was not out of his home territory might well have been carrying no more than the thirty-odd.

Handling the body presented difficulties I hadn't foreseen. After all, he had been a little, old guy and pretty much dried out—no fat on him and not much muscle. If he would weigh a hundred and twenty, it would be a lot. I'd lifted the body with Stan when we had taken him out of the car, but it hadn't needed the two of us. He was that small and light.

This time, however, it wasn't as easy. Rigor had set in and was fully developed. At low temperatures it develops quickly and it's a longer time passing off. The rigid body was difficult. I thought of going back to the house and pulling Dawson away from Doris Day to help with it, but I didn't. I guess I was showing off a little. I was being Sally Sobieski's cavalier and who ever heard of a cavalier's assistant?

I had to juggle a bit to get it made, but I did it without trailing the body in the snow or offering it any other indignities. Back in the house Sally had covered the table with a lace cloth and she was waiting with another cloth that would be for covering the body. Mr. Hoffman was going to be laid out in fitting style.

I was wondering what Stan was saying about the old man on his visits to the police barracks. He was certainly making some sort of report of the old man's death. He'd mentioned it to the man at the dairy. He could hardly be leaving it for local gossip to bring it to the ears of the cops.

I laid the body on the lace cloth. Sally made a try at arranging it in what she must have been thinking would be a suitable funerary attitude, but the rigor, of course, defeated her. Her eyes filled with tears.

"I didn't know him well," she said, "but he was sweet. I wish I had some flowers or something."

I took the second cloth and covered the body, drawing the cloth up over the face. She moved to turn it back but, thinking better of it, she stepped away. I took her by the hand and led her out of the cold room. In the doorway she paused and looked back at the table. I waited for her out in the hall and, when she joined me there, I shut the door behind her.

Out in the hall we could hear the TV. Doris Day was taking time out for the commercials. That kid was back on, the one who took such good care of herself that she was staving off senility at twenty-one. We went in there. The TV was doing its stuff for an empty room. Sally switched it off and went out to the foot of the stairs.

"Bert?" she called. "Are you up there? What are you doing?"

It was a few moments before he answered.

"Your towel," he said, shouting down from the head of the stairs. "I'm trying to wash the stuff out of it."

She told him not to bother.

"Just come on down and bring it with you," she said. "I'll throw it in the washing machine. I'm going to do a wash anyhow. I'll be running out of things for Firpo if I don't."

Dawson came down with the stained and dripping bath towel. She took it from him.

"You know what she did?" he said. "Did Matt tell you? She had the nerve to say you locked her up without anything to eat. She said I never brought her anything. She called me a liar."

"That's nothing to all the other things she called us," Sally said. "All I want is to forget her."

It wasn't to be that easily done. When Stan got back, he was carrying souvenirs of the lady. He had a nasty scratch down one side of his face and a couple more on the backs of his hands. He said they were nothing but Sally insisted on washing them and she made him hold still for iodine.

"That woman is poison," she said. "Who knows what she carries on her claws?"

She insisted on knowing what had happened.

"She was okay all the way in," Stan said. "You know how it is with the noise. You can't talk or anyway you can't hear. She just stayed quiet and did nothing."

Sally was working on the scratches.

"Nothing," she growled.

"That was later, when we got there," Stan explained. "It was when she saw it was the police barracks. I guess she'd thought I was taking them to a motel or something. Matt was writing off his two hundred bucks and I was just going to forget what they tried with the snowmobile. I suppose she'd even been thinking they had us fooled on who they are. When she saw it was the police barracks, she went crazy. The cops had to come out and pull her off me."

"Did they open the suitcase?" Dawson asked.

"She had the key," Stan said. "The fellows found it in her purse and they got the thing unlocked."

"Bearer bonds?" I asked.

"Yeah, them. Them and money, about five thousand in hundreds and fifties."

Dawson turned to me.

"You said yours was tens and twenties," he said.

"They're figuring what they had in the suitcase was from the bank," Stan said. "He had about a hundred on him in tens and fives and singles. She had over two hundred in her purse. At least two hundred of that was in the tens and twenties."

Sally finished working on the scratches. She kissed him—his hands and his face. He might have been Firpo. She was kissing the scratches to make them better.

"You need a drink," she said. "We all need a drink."

I poured them out and we drank to fair weather. The prediction had been more heavy snow and this time the weather kids had it right.

"In the suitcase," Dawson asked, "did they find anything else in there?"

"Just clothes," Stan said. "Shirts, underwear, stuff like that. It was on top with the money and the bonds underneath."

"Nothing else?"

Dawson seemed disappointed.

"What else would there be?" Stan asked him.

"I don't know. I thought maybe something they'd ripped off from old man Hoffman."

"Yeah," Stan sighed. "I know what you mean, but nothing unless it was that they took some of the money off Hoffman and there's no way of knowing that."

"If there was money missing from the bank along with the bonds," Sally suggested, "the bank would know and, if the money in the suitcase is more than the bank is short . . ."

"It still wouldn't mean anything," I said. "They could have had some money of their own. It wasn't as though they could have been planning on ever going back. They wouldn't have left anything."

There was no arguing it. Nothing could have been more reasonable, but that didn't make them like it. Dawson looked disappointed. Sally looked unhappy. Stan was harder to read. He was studying my face, and I could see nothing in his but distress. We dropped it.

"Did you remember to get me the gas?" Dawson asked.

"Yeah. On the way back I stopped by your place and left it there."

"How did you get in?"

"How do you think I got in? I busted a window and went in that way. Stop being an old woman. I left the can by the door to the garage. You may have to dig it out of the snow, but it's there, just by the garage door."

Dawson relaxed.

"What do I owe you?" he asked.

"Nothing," Stan said. "We'll call it what we siphoned out of your pickup."

Dawson went along on that. It seemed cheap to me.

"I been thinking," Dawson said. "It's time I went back home. With the power on, it'll be okay over there. I'll have the TV and I won't be stuck like I was before. I can get the snowmobile gassed up and get around. It's time you people had your place to yourselves."

"How will you be for food?" Sally asked. "You brought your supplies over here."

"Only the milk and the little I could carry," Dawson said. "I get the snowmobile going again, I can go for milk and anything else I need. That's no problem."

"You could come over here to eat," Sally offered. "You're always welcome."

"I'll do that sometimes. Let me know when you're cooking something special good."

"That's all the time," Stan said.

"I'll just mush across and gas up the snowmobile," Dawson said. "Then I'll come back and get Matt."

"Stan will run you over," Sally offered.

"What do you mean get Matt?" Stan asked.

"Like the man said," I told him, "it's time you had your house to yourself."

"We have plenty of beds," Stan said. "You stay here."

"He'll be all right with me," Dawson said.

The two men went off with the argument unsettled.

Sally laughed.

"That Bert Dawson," she said after they'd gone. "He's a funny one. He hasn't any reason for not going home but he doesn't want to be there alone. When the roads are open, he's always racketing around all over the place; but with this snow tying everybody down, he's going to be lonely. He's like a kid."

I laughed with her.

"Half kid and half old woman," I said.

"I don't know," Sally murmured. "Maybe he's right to lock up with people like those Kings around."

"In this snow?"

"In any weather," Sally said. "That witch, all she'd need is to find a broomstick handy."

"She wasn't carrying one," I said.

I was thinking about the old man's body across the hall in the unheated room. Since the Kings were almost certainly guilty of the bank job, very likely guilty of lifting my two hundred bucks, and indisputably guilty of the hijacking attempt on the snowmobile, nothing could have made a neater package than dumping the old man's murder on them as well. It was neat enough, to be sure, but snow and geography stood in the way. I was also disposed to add motive.

The Kings weren't locals. It was not likely that they would have known that Hoffman was in the diamond business and that he would have been likely to be carrying diamonds or a large sum of cash or both. Their car got stuck in the snow nowhere near the spot where the old man's wheels had stopped rolling and they'd had no means of moving over the considerable distance that lay between those two places on those two roads.

There was also the snowmobile that had come close to me and had gone away. And the car door that had been dug out only a short time before I came on it. There was also the dispatch case that had been returned to the car some time during the night, a time that came after our removal of the body.

I could stretch and make that last item work out for one of the Kings. He could have sneaked out during the night and taken the snowmobile to make it over there and back without waking anyone, but even as I was trying to work that out, I knew that I couldn't make it stick.

I was remembering that Stan had said that after making that last trip to bring me to the house, the snowmobile had been all but out of gas. He had been right about that, since there hadn't been enough for even the short run across to Bert Dawson's place. The gas, of course, could have been brought down that low by an additional trip made with the dispatch case during the night, but that would mean Stan had lied about when the gas dropped down to that almost useless level. It made no sense to think that he would have told that lie if that final trip had not been his own.

There was just no way the Hoffman thing could have been pinned on the Kings. There had never been the first reason for suspecting them of it beyond the simple thought that crimes are committed by criminals and we knew them to be criminals. That's the kind of thinking cops do when they look around the vicinity of a crime and round up all the neighborhood characters who have records. It's police routine, of course, but most of the time they have to turn all those characters loose. They find no reason to hold them.

I could think of only one more thing and on that I was reaching. There had been Mrs. King's reaction of hysterical distress when Stan brought the murdered man's body home. I wasn't ready to believe that her nerves were as bad as she constantly proclaimed them to be, but obviously she had more than a little to be nervous about and it didn't need a murder to add up to that more than a little. But nobody could call her nerves evidence.

So there I was back to Stan Sobieski, good husband, good father, all-around good guy, and not excluding good neighbor. The more I had been seeing of the man, and we could hardly have been living at closer quarters, the less I was able to hang onto the belief that he could be a murderer. He had the strength for it and the heft, but having it is one thing; using it on a little old man and doing it in cold blood has to be something else again.

I told myself that one never knew. It was always possible to be mistaken about a man. Character reading is nobody's exact science. I couldn't say that I had taken a liking to Melvin King or had ever thought too well of him, but I'd had him pegged for an ineffectual little slob, all fat and fatuousness. A man can fool you about himself even when he has no great stake in fooling you. When everything hangs on his bringing it off and he's in there working at it, he can snow you but good.

But absconding from the bank with those bearer bonds, there couldn't be a dopier crime than that. Then there had been the try he made at grabbing the snowmobile. That one was an idiot's crime. Even if he thought they could hold the lot of us off with his pistol, where could they have gone? Was he going to snowmobile all the way to the border and across into Canada?

The only thing that put the least bit of sense into that caper was desperation. We had pinned the ripoff of my two hundred pretty well to his wife. If we handed her over to the police and charged her with the theft, they would be up the creek right there.

I could see where he'd felt that they had to get away from us and make it to some place where nobody would have any ideas of handing them over to the cops.

With the TV news giving out about the bank deal and the likelihood that they'd soon have the additional news that a couple answering the King description had picked a man's pocket for two hundred dollars and taken off on a stolen snowmobile, it wouldn't have been long before people would have noticed. Even a desperate man should have realized that he was piling crime on crime without the first chance of doing himself any good. I hadn't been all that wrong when I'd pegged the guy for an ineffectual fool.

IX

Stan came back. He didn't look happy. He was at least as tense and uncomfortable as he had been when he'd had the job of taking the Kings to the police. From the way he looked and acted I thought he might have been at the point of loading me on his snowmobile to make his third trip of carrying criminal freight to the police barracks.

I more than half expected him to tell me to get my coat and come along, but he didn't.

"Bert'll be over to pick you up," he said. "He's gone into town first to get more gas and some supplies. He'll be over for you when he gets back."

"He could have taken me with him to help him tote," I said. "It's time you people had me out of your hair."

"Nonsense, Matt," Sally said. "I don't know how we'd ever have managed without you."

"You and Stan," I said. "You'd have managed all right."

"I don't know," Stan said. "It was you had all the ideas, using the grill, siphoning the gas out of the cars. I don't know how long I'd have been before I thought of anything like that, if I ever would have."

He was pacing the room, talking with his back to me. I had a feeling that he was avoiding meeting my eye.

"You'd have thought of something," I said. "Necessity is the mother of invention and all that jazz."

We were making conversation. It's never good conversation when it doesn't just come and it has to be made.

"You had the ideas," Stan said. "You had them in time and they worked. That's all I know. I wish I knew some way I could show you how much I appreciate it."

It was crazy, but he seemed to be waiting for me to tell him that he could show his appreciation by just forgetting about me and the little, old guy we had laid out across the hall. I said nothing and for several moments there was dead silence. He broke it by going to the TV and turning it on.

He got a football game. They were playing in Miami. Nothing could have looked more unreal than the guys along the sidelines sweaty in their short-sleeved sports shirts and the guys out on the field with their eyes blacked up to protect them against sun glare. We were in a world that looked as though it had never seen the sun.

I suppose it was a good enough game. I watched it but I couldn't keep my mind on it and it was obvious that it was the same with Stan. If anybody was enjoying it, it was Sally for the parts of it she watched between the various household chores she was doing. She knew football. She'd been hooked on the game ever since high school. I gathered that it had been back then that she'd gotten hooked on Stan Sobieski. He'd been a defensive linebacker.

She still had the shiner. It looked better than it had when I had first seen it, but it still had a long way to go. They don't disappear in a day. I just couldn't picture her as the kind of girl who would stay with a guy if he ever beat up on her, but then I hadn't the first idea of how much a woman would take when she loved a guy like that.

I was wishing Dawson would get there and pull me out of it. I even had the thought that I might head over to his place on the skis, but there was the question of how Stan would take that. There was also the possibility that I'd get over there and find the place all locked up and Dawson not yet back from town.

The waiting was strained and it grew steadily more uncomfortable. As long as the Kings had been there, any tension there might have been between Stan and me had dropped into the background: it had been us against them. Now it was what he was thinking and what I was thinking and only the one thing in both our minds.

The game was well into the last quarter when Sally came in from the kitchen and said there'd be supper as soon as the game finished. Stan said he could shut it off; she didn't have to hold supper, but she said supper would wait. She wanted to sit awhile and watch the rest of it. At the final whistle Stan switched the set off.

"You boys want a drink?" Sally asked.

"What about you girls?" I asked her.

"Why do you think I brought it up?" she said.

Stan poured. He walked past my Virginia Gentleman— there was still one of the quarts untouched—and went to bring out his own booze. It looked as though he was throwing me a signal but I didn't know how I was to pick it up. Even while he was pouring, we heard the snowmobile. Dawson came in. He brought with him a beer breath that met the smells of Sally's cooking head on and simply wiped them out.

He was full of sudsy good cheer.

"Just in time for a chaser," he said. "How's that for timing?"

"Lousy," Stan said, as he brought out another glass and poured Dawson his chaser.

"We're just sitting down to supper," Sally said. "I'll put out another plate. You'll eat with us."

"Call that lousy timing, Stan?" Dawson chortled.

"I'm cursed with a hospitable wife," Stan said.

We went to the table. Dawson kept a line of nonsense going all the time we ate. Stan kept his eyes fixed on his plate and ate in dogged silence. Sally kept the talk going with Dawson. In the chitchat department I wasn't any better than Stan. I'm sure the supper was good, but it was wasted on me. I didn't know what I was eating.

As soon as we'd finished, Dawson pulled away from the table.

"You won't tell anybody that we ate and ran," he said.

"Sit awhile," Sally urged.

Stan wasn't backing her up on it. He went out and came back with my coat. He also brought me the untouched quart of whiskey.

"You keep that," I said.

"I've got some."

He pushed it at me.

"Bert doesn't need it," I said. "He's got a skinful now."

I was shrugging into my coat. Stan was scowling. He rammed the bottle down into the pocket of my sheepskin. He put so much force into it that, catching me in mid-shrug, he hauled the coat down off my shoulders. He caught at it and hauled it back up again and he again put so much force into it that he might have been trying to lift me off my feet and hoist me by my coat. You can call it speeding the parting guest. It felt like the bum's rush.

He said some sort of a good-by and Sally did a better job of it, but he had us out of there and on Dawson's snowmobile in nothing flat. The short ride over to Dawson's place was like all the snowmobile rides, noise, wind, snow, and no possibility of talk.

Dawson left me standing by his house door while he put the snowmobile into the garage. It took him a little time. He had to unlock the garage door, shove the thing in, and then lock the garage door after it. I tried the house door. It was locked. I had to wait for him to come over with the key.

He opened up and we went in. He had his furnace pouring heat. At that moment, when we were coming in out of the cold, it felt all right, but I knew it wasn't going to be long before that heat would be cooking us. I thought about the bag I had sitting in Baby's trunk. I wished I had it with me. There was stuff in there I could have changed into. Inside the thermal long johns I was going to come to a quick boil.

"You want all this much heat?" I asked.

"I like a warm house," he said.

It was his house. Nothing to be done about that. I did what I could. I hauled out of the sheepskin. I pulled off the sweater. I took off the lumberjack shirt.

He had a small place and it was furnished like a barracks, but it would never have passed a barracks inspection. It wasn't dirty, but the way he'd been making the bed over at the Sobieskis should have been the tipoff: it was sloppy. When I took my things off and looked around for a place to put them, he told me to just drop them anywhere and make myself at home. Obviously that was the way he did things. I could see the stuff he had just dropped anywhere. There was a shoe under a chair one side of the room and its mate under the television stand on the other side. A shirt hung from one of the posts of a chair back. There were some socks here and there, lying on the floor.

He switched the TV on and fiddled with the knobs till he

had what he wanted, one of those old Westerns nobody ever saw when it was in the theaters because everybody knew better.

"Sit down," he said, "and watch the Apaches get knocked off."

It was the typical TV evening. At the commercial breaks, he would nip out to his kitchen and bring back two cans of beer, one for me and one for himself.

The Western came to its end. The cowboy got the school-marm and the Indians got the U. S. Cavalry. Dawson twiddled the knobs, settling for a give-away show where people jumped up and down in mad ecstasy at winning a microwave oven and twenty cases of toilet paper.

Dawson left it on. But since he found it something less than absorbing, he took to talking over it.

"That Sobieski," he said. "That's one flaky guy. He's killing himself worrying about you. His trouble is he's got a conscience and he hasn't got the guts he needs for living with it."

"How's that?" I asked.

"He's got it in his head that you killed the old guy, Hoffman. He says he's got to tell the cops what he knows. It's his duty. But he's been into the police barracks twice today with them King crooks and he hasn't said anything about you yet."

"Did he tell you why he hasn't?" I asked.

"He says he can't go saying anything like that about a man, he may be innocent. He's got to be sure first. Crazy."

"How is he going to make sure?"

"He's going to wait until we can get into your car. We're going to make you open it up—the trunk, the glove compartment, under the seats, everything. The old man was in the diamond business and Stan figures he was carrying diamonds and that was what he was killed for. We find diamonds stowed some place in your car, he'll be sure."

"And if you don't find any diamonds?" I said.

"He'll be where he is now, not knowing what to do. He don't know whether he wants to find the diamonds in your car or not. If he finds them, he can do what he says he's got to do and not sweat about it so much, though you saw him, he sweated plenty when he took the Kings in and he didn't have no doubts about them."

"What do you think?" I asked.

"Me?" Dawson said, talking past a yawn. "I think Stan Sobieski's out of his skull."

"Who do you think killed the old man?"

"Nobody killed him. He got stuck in the snow and he tried to make it on foot. You know how it was out there. He was little and old and feeble. How could he battle that wind?"

"But you think he tried it anyhow?"

"Sure, he tried it. He tried it and he fell and knocked his head. He dragged himself back to the car. He'd have been half knocked out and more than half frozen. So he did what he'd never have done if he was in his right mind. He rolled the windows up tight and he got the heater going. It was either the monoxide got him or he had a heart attack. Nobody killed him."

"That wasn't the way it happened," I said. "It couldn't have been that way."

"Why not? Tell me why not."

"When I found him, he didn't have the motor running and the key wasn't in the ignition."

"So what? Maybe he remembered about the monoxide. Once he got the car warm, he turned off the motor and took the key out of the ignition. You can figure it was the last thing the poor old guy did, but he was too late. The car was full of fumes unless, like I said, it was a heart attack. An old guy like him, cold and scared. He was a cinch for a heart attack."

"Okay. Where did he put the key?"

"In his pocket."

"But he didn't. That's what got Stan to thinking about me. Didn't he tell you?"

"He told me," Dawson said.

I went through the whole key business for him and he'd heard it all from Stan Sobieski. He poohpoohed the whole thing.

"It was there all the time," he said. "You just missed it the first time you looked."

"I checked all his pockets," I said.

"By feel," he argued, "in the dark in that freezing barn. So your hands get so cold, they don't feel anything. You just missed finding them. It don't mean a thing."

"When I found him," I said, trying it from another angle, "the snow was drifted up solid around his car. You had to dig it away to get to where you could open the doors, but there was the one door on the side where the drifting was heaviest. I opened that one without any trouble. Somebody had been there before me and had dug that door out."

"The old man himself. He'd have to so he could get himself back into the car."

"How could he stand against the wind? He was half knocked out from hitting his head, but he had the strength for digging his way in?"

Dawson shrugged.

"He used up his last strength getting himself back into the

car. That alone was enough to give him a heart attack. Young guys, strong and healthy, drop dead shoveling their driveways. It happens all the time."

I shook my head.

"No good," I said. "Let's say that somehow he did find the strength to do it. He gets back in the car. He sits there long enough for the monoxide to get to him. Then he sits in there long enough for his body to go cold. He was cold when I found him and the snow was drifting fast, but all the same, the door wasn't drifted over. Somebody opened that door a good long while after the old man was past doing anything. Maybe he wasn't dead yet but he would have been at least near it."

We stood even. I wasn't selling him my version either.

"It don't mean anything," he said. "It'll turn out some guy was out on his snowmobile looking for people who were stuck. He finds the old man but it's too late, so he shuts the door and leaves him to go off and look for somebody who's maybe not past helping. Maybe the guy will turn up to report it and maybe he'll never say anything about it. He'll be ashamed."

"Did Stan tell you about the dispatch case?" I asked.

"Yeah, he told me."

"You think we imagined that?"

He agreed that we couldn't have imagined it, but he had an easy answer for it.

"You read the papers," he said. "You listen to the TV news. Every time there's a disaster, a fire or an earthquake or a riot or anything, you get looters. It's happened in cities all over the place, so it happens here too. This blizzard is a disaster. You listen to the news, you'll hear it. There's talk of naming Buffalo a disaster area. Some bastard finds the car with the dead old man in it. He sees the dispatch case and he thinks he'll rip it off. Then he can't get it unlocked and he gets to thinking it's a bad idea. He goes and puts it back."

I had one more item sitting in my head, the snowmobile that came close and had its light turned full on me and then just turned and blasted away from there. I hadn't told Stan Sobieski about that. I was wondering whether I should bring it up now. While I was thinking about it, Dawson had another idea.

"You say somebody got the car door open after the old man was dead," he said. "Maybe the dispatch case proves it. The guy dug his way in and got the door open. He finds old man Hoffman dead or dying and he sees the case there on the seat beside him. He grabs it and takes off. That makes sense, doesn't it?"

"If it made sense to his way of thinking, it seemed to me that it made better sense to mine. It explained the mistake the man had made, putting the case in the only place it could not have been when we took the body out of the car. He put it back where he had found it, thinking that he was fixing it so that it would look as though it had never been touched.

Dawson pulled to his feet and switched off the TV.

"How's for some shuteye?" he said.

"Where do I sleep?" I asked.

"There's only the one bed," he said.

"Then I'll be all right here in the chair. You go on to bed."

"No," Dawson said.

"Yes," I insisted. "I'm not putting you out of your bed."

"Like you did with Stan. We share it."

It wasn't at all like. At the Sobieskis it had been in a room full of people and there had been no heat except from the fire. We'd slept with all our clothes on.

"No, thanks," I said.

"Hey, man," he said. "What do you take me for?"

"Just no thanks."

"Was you ever in the Army?" he asked.

"I was. So what?"

"When you were on a shipment, remember? Overnight on a train, it was always one man in an upper berth and two in the lower, and the bed's bigger than any lower berth."

"I missed that," I said. "I was brass. I rated a berth to my-self."

He gave that the GI touch.

"So tonight you'll be just ordinary common folks, not different from any dogface."

"Forget it," I said. "The chair will do me fine."

"I can't forget it. I promised Sobieski."

"You promised him what?"

"I'd keep an eye on you, day and night. That's why we fixed it this way with me and you over here. It was so I could take over on watching you and he could get to sleep with his wife."

"But you don't think I need to be watched. Isn't that what you've been telling me?"

"It makes no difference what I think. I swore to Stan."

"Do you have to tell him?"

"Look," he said. "It's all right for you. Another day, two days, the road will be cleared and you'll take off. I live here. Stan and me, we're neighbors, buddies. I can't lie to him."

It was crazy, but I was stuck with it. Also I was feeling a fool, like a girl in a Victorian novel, fighting for her virginity. I gave up.

We went into the bedroom. I undressed. He left his stuff lying wherever he had dropped it. Out of habit—I'm well trained—I headed for the closet. I was going to hang the stuff up, but the closet door was locked, and he made no move to unlock it.

He stretched and yawned.

"Just put them anywhere," he said.

We had been calling him an old woman because of all his locking up. Now he was making me feel like the old woman, a guy with fussy habits.

"When in Rome," I thought.

I just dropped all my things where I stood.

It was a small room. The bed was against the wall.

"You get in," he said. "I'm just going to the john."

I wondered whether that was the way the bed always stood or if it had been moved to the wall for purposes of my captivity. Obviously he was going to have me where I couldn't get out without climbing over him. I stayed away from the bed and waited for him to come back. There are a lot of breaks for commercials in a TV evening and there had been all those beers. He was right about the john. You know how it is with beer. You don't buy it. You only rent it.

He came back and I took my turn. It was right next to the bedroom and I'd seen the way he went. I needed no guidance, particularly since he had left the door open while he was in there. Whether I needed it or not, he came along ostensibly to show me the way and he stood in the doorway waiting for me. When I came out, he stepped aside and waited for me to go back into the bedroom ahead of him. It wasn't courtly manners. It was the way he was setting it up. He was going to have me against the wall.

It was stifling in there.

"Don't you turn the heat down for the night?" I asked.

"I like it warm," he said.

"Fuel crisis."

"Screw it. I like it warm."

"What about a little open window?"

I wanted to come out of that night alive.

"With the mercury falling out of the bottom of the thermometer?" he said. "Are you crazy, man?"

"We'll suffocate."

"It's those drawers you've got on," he said.

If I was feeling the heat, it was to be my own fault.

"I know," I said. "I should have dressed for your house. I came unprepared."

"You can have a pair of my jockeys if you want," he offered.

"I want," I said. "Thanks."

"Okay," he said. "Come and get them."

He led the way out through the other room and on into his kitchen. He had a washer and dryer in there. Opening the dryer, he fished out a pair of briefs and tossed them at me. Evidently that was the way he lived. He never put anything away. When he ran his stuff through the washer, he just left it lying in the dryer till he wanted it. Nothing wrong with that, I was telling myself. It was as good as a bureau drawer. I just wondered why he didn't have a padlock on the dryer.

Back in the bedroom, he stood over me and watched me while I changed into the jockeys. He was going to such extremes in keeping his promise to Stan that he was turning it into a farce.

"Now are you ready?" he asked.

I was keeping him up.

I thought I wasn't going to sleep, but the beer did its work on me and I did sleep. It wasn't one of those good nights of unbroken sleep. It was too hot and stuffy in there for that. He got up once during the night and, although from the way he moved I knew he was trying to do it without waking me, it was when I happened to be awake.

He was out what seemed to be a long time, but I remembered that he'd had a good head start on the beers. I was surprised that he hadn't roused me and taken me with him.

In the morning I was awake before him. My head felt as though it had grown to twice its normal size and had filled up with glue. The wall I was up against had a window in it and the glass gleamed brilliantly white. I reached up and touched it. The feel of it against my fingers was wonderful. It was cold. I scratched at its coating of frost crystals and cleared a space I could see through. It was blinding outside. The snow had stopped. The sky was blue and cloudless. With the morning sun on it, the snow cover was dazzling.

There was only the one thing I needed in the world and that was to be out in it. The air out there would be clean and cold and fresh and in every part of me I ached for it. I wanted the chill of it in my nostrils. I wanted to suck it down into my lungs. I had to breathe it if I was ever to clear my head. If the torrid miasma of that house had seemed unendurable before this, now it was unendurable and no seeming about it.

I tried to pull up carefully and climb over him without waking him, but obviously it was impossible. He woke just as I was stepping over him. He grabbed me by the ankle.

"The john?" he asked.

"Some fresh air," I said. "I have to get outside."

"Outside? In the snow and the cold?"

"I'm going out."

"Stan," he reminded me.

"That's between you and Stan," I said. "If you hurry, you can come out with me."

"It's cold out there."

"It's stinking in here."

"After breakfast."

I jerked my ankle free of his grip.

"Right now."

"Take a cold shower if you want," he said.

"Right now I don't want anything but cold air."

I was pulling on my socks.

"Jesus," he grumbled, but he started hurrying into his clothes.

All I did was haul on my boots. I started out of the room.

"Hey." He came hopping after me, one leg in his pants and the other out. "You're not going out that way?"

"Relax," I said. "How far can I get this way?"

I kept going. On the way through the other room, I picked up my sheepskin and shrugged into it. Just for stepping out the door to learn how it would feel to breathe again, it was all I needed. The way I was feeling, I didn't need even that. I was having a dream of rolling in the snow buck naked. They tell you that hell is a hot place but they never say about heaven. I was thinking then that heaven had to be a cold place, otherwise Erridge wasn't going to want it. I got as far as the door and there I had to wait for him. It was locked and he wasn't coming to unlock it until he was back in all his clothes and had bundled up.

Waiting with that sheepskin on me was too much. I took it off. By that time I was yelling for him to hurry it up and he was telling me to keep my pants on. He was finally ready and he unlocked the door.

I pushed past him and I did it. I dove into the snow and rolled in it. I whooped and I yelled and I filled my lungs. It was one of the great moments of my life.

"You're crazy," he said, and he went back into the house leaving me to my cavorting.

I had found the limits of the promise he had made to Stan Sobieski. He didn't have to stay out there and watch me. My skis were with his snowmobile locked away in the garage. My clothes were in the house and with them my credit cards and the few bucks in change that was all that was left to me in the way of cash.

Even he and his buddy, Stan, could have no worry about my going anywhere and he didn't need to worry about my making off with the pair of jockeys he'd lent me.

I went back into the house, glowing all over and with my head clear. It was more than clear. I felt as though I had just repossessed it. I was wondering where it had been for a day and more.

X

Inside I headed for the bathroom to towel myself down. He came with me. He'd made certain that I wouldn't be coming back into the house without his knowing it. When he'd gone in and left me in the snow, he had locked the house door. I'd had to pound on it to get him to come and let me in.

"We'll go out to the kitchen," he said. "I'm fixing breakfast."

You may be thinking that with me next to naked, he could have been keeping his promise to Stan even though for a moment or two he let me get out of his sight, as he had just done out in the snow. I was past thinking that. I knew that inside the house was different. Inside the house I needed watching.

He'd wheeled the TV into the kitchen. I've never known a guy more addicted. He put on coffee. He made toast. He fried eggs. He boiled the coffee. He burned the toast. He broke the egg yolks and he scorched the whites. He did everything wrong. Guys who live alone don't get to be automatic Escoffiers but they usually develop some rudimentary kitchen skills just from doing it every day. Dawson was operating as though he had never seen a stove before.

He scraped the eggs off the pan onto a couple of plates. The way he'd done them, they wouldn't come off without scraping. He left it to me to scrape the charcoal off my own toast. I could just as well have left it on because the coffee tasted as though it had been made out of the toast scrapings.

That wasn't just an unpalatable breakfast. It was a disgusting one, but he tucked into his and my roll in the snow had given me an appetite. I wolfed mine down. When food is that bad, you have to wolf it. You don't want it hanging around in your mouth long enough for the taste buds to get a good whack at it.

The morning news was on and for the first time it was sounding good. It was still mostly about the snow, but there had been a change. They were promising that the sun would stay with us. The work of clearing the roads had begun. They were warning that it was going to take time. The cars abandoned along the roads were slowing up the snowplows, but things were opening up. The runways at the local airport had been swept clean and traffic in and out had resumed. The area was no longer isolated.

The rest of it was estimates of the damage—so many known deaths directly attributable to the snow and the cold, so many man hours of work lost with workers unable to get to the plants, so much lost in production. Dawson got up from the table and did something I'd never thought I'd see him do. He switched off the TV. He had something to say and it was important. He wanted to be sure of my full attention.

"The airport's this side of town," he said. "It's right near here. The way it is now with the snow stopped and no wind and the sun out, you could get on your skis and make it over there easy."

This could have been a prelude to telling me that with this change in the weather he was going to have to keep me locked in the bedroom or tied up or something like that, but I didn't think it was going to be that. I said nothing and waited for him to go on.

"You can ski over there and hop the first plane out, any plane, wherever it's going. Stan's going to go to the cops and he's going to tell them his crazy story, they'll have to pick you up. Of course, they won't hold you for long, but it's bound to be a while. It'll be till they get the cars dug out, the old man's and yours, and till they get the body into the hospital and do an autopsy and find how he died."

He paused, waiting for me to say something. I said nothing. He could think I was a slow study. I wanted him to go on with it. I wanted him to draw diagrams for me.

"It'll be a couple of days anyhow," he said, "and though I guess no jail's a Hilton hotel, this one here, I wouldn't wish it on a dog. I was in it once for a night, so I know what I'm talking about. I had maybe a beer or two too many and I was driving home when they hauled me for driving under the influence. Under the influence? Between you and me, I was stoned. Even the way I was, though, I knew it was no Hilton hotel."

I could have told him that Hiltons weren't Erridge's style, but I wasn't going to interrupt the flow.

"You know how to get to the dairy," he said. "You went there with Stan. You take that same turnoff like going to the dairy, but you take it only a hundred and fifty or maybe two hundred yards. Before you hit the gas station, you'll see a road going off to the left. That's the airport road, and once you're on it, you're almost there."

I had been waiting for him to draw me diagrams. A little more and he would have been drawing me a map.

"Since the airport's open and they're flying in and out of it," he said, "the plows must have been through there. So by the time you hit the airport road, you won't even need the skis. You can just walk in."

He stopped again, waiting for me to say something. I said nothing.

"Look," he said. "How about it? You can do it easy, but you've got to do it right away. You've got to be on a plane and away from here before Stan goes sounding off to the police. Sure, he'll make a fool of himself, but in the meantime you'll be having a couple of bad days."

"What do you do about your promise to Stan?" I asked.

"I'll tell him I had to go and, while I was in the john, you got away from me. Even the dumbest Polack knows that. A guy's got to go some time."

"You said you couldn't lie to him."

"Hell. There's always got to be a first time. He'll get to know how close he came to making an ass of himself and he'll be happy you got away from me and saved him from it. It'll be okay between me and Stan."

I pushed away from the table.

"I've done my share of jail time," I said. "First over at the Sobieskis with Stan riding my tail and last night here with you. Just give me those directions again. I go out to the road and take it past where the old man got stuck and past my car."

He broke in on me.

"Is that where it happened to him?" he exclaimed. "That close to here? The poor old guy, if he could only have made it this far. To come that close, it's awful."

"Didn't you know?"

"How was I to know? You know how I was caught when the snow came with no gas in the snowmobile tank. I thought of going out on the snowshoes, but what could I do on those? I couldn't bring anybody in and I figured the guys, with their snowmobiles going would all be out. Besides, like you see, I just can't take the cold."

I could have asked him how come a guy with his passion for keeping warm even owned a snowmobile and a pair of snowshoes, but that wouldn't have been playing along and I was playing along. I took him back to his road directions. He repeated them for me and all the time he was talking, I was listening hard. He was giving me the distances and they were all short distances. I wasn't just listening to his directions. I was listening for planes. In all the time I had been there, first at the Sobieski house and now in his, I had never once heard a plane. Okay. The airport had been snowed in. No planes had been flying, but now the airport had been opened. If he lived as close as he said, I'd be hearing planes.

This was a trap and I knew it was, but I was going to walk —or ski—right into it. There was an airport, I knew that from the TV, but it wasn't anywhere near where he was telling me to go.

This bastard thought he was going to get me sucked into running. He was going to let me start out and then he was going to hop his snowmobile and take off to the police barracks. He would tell them how I got away from him because he had to go to the john and he'd tell them the direction I'd gone.

I could hear the story he'd feed them, how I'd asked him a lot of questions about where the airport was and, since he hadn't trusted me, he'd told me the wrong direction. He'd tell them I was out there on my skis looking for the airport and they'd go out and get me.

He had been working on this all night. Nobody lived the way he said he did, not in a steaming house with no air. All that had been for me, and the breakfast, too. He'd been pushing me to the place where, even though I'd never touched the old man or his diamonds and I had no reason to run, I'd be grasping at anything that would deliver me from spending even another hour in this hellhole he'd set up for me.

It was okay. He was giving me the right directions. All I had to do was ignore this second turnoff he was feeding me. I knew the way. It would be past the gas station and on past the dairy. I remembered it from what Stan Sobieski had said. The police barracks was on that road this side of the town. The cops weren't going to go out and find me. I was going to go in and find them.

If he was that quick and they were that quick, they might, of course, come out and pick me up before I got to the barracks, but that wouldn't matter. I had the whole thing. I had it all wrapped up and ready to hand it to them.

There had been the one piece of it all the time that I'd never thought to fit in. There had been the overwhelming stink of gas in the locked-up garage and the snowmobile not merely with its tank so low that it would have been no use trying to go anywhere on it, but absolutely and completely dry.

Have you ever run out of gas? If you're lucky, you're on a well-traveled road where you can pick up a lift to where you can get a canful and bring it back and pour it into your tank to take you to the nearest pump so you can get filled up. If you're not so lucky, it'll be where you're going to have a long hike before you get to any place where you can buy some. It's not likely that you'll ever have just exactly enough to carry you precisely to your garage. Not in a million years is it going to feed its last drop as you come through the garage door. Nobody can be that lucky.

The way that garage had been filled up with fumes I'd

been certain that he had a leak in the tank on his pickup and I was going to find all the gas drained away, but there hadn't been any leak. He had gone out on his snowmobile and he had picked up the old man. He was going to rescue him. He was going to take him home to his house where they would sit out the blizzard cozy and warm together. Once he had the old guy out of the car, he blipped him on the head and dropped him unconscious in the snow. Then he loaded him back behind the wheel, rolled the windows up tight, got the motor running, and left the old man shut up in there to die.

I was remembering something else. I was remembering the way the old man's car had been sitting there in the snow. It hadn't been straightaway as Baby had been when we got stuck. It had been slewed diagonally across the road. It hadn't been running into a drift that had stopped the old man. He'd gone into a skid and it had scared him. He had been afraid to drive farther. With the car sitting at that angle, its headlights had been pointed at Dawson's house. Dawson had seen them and had zipped over on his snowmobile to investigate. The drifts I'd seen had built around the car while the old man had been in there, first dying and then dead. Dawson had given him plenty of time.

Then he'd returned on his snowmobile. By then the snow had drifted against the car doors. He dug the one door out and opened it and checked. The old man was dead. He turned off the engine and took the keys. He needed them because among them on the ring was the key to the dispatch case and he didn't dare stand out there on the road fiddling it off the ring. I knew why he didn't dare stand out there then. The light on his snowmobile had picked me up. I was too close, and with the skis I could be coming closer.

He took off back to his house where he unlocked the case

and emptied it. He probably would have liked to take the empty case right back to the car and set it on the seat beside the old man. And he would have wanted to put the car key back into the ignition and set the motor to running again. That would have made the picture perfect for him, the old man dead in the car with the windows all tight and the motor running.

He couldn't do it. From the house he would have seen Stan's snowmobile light and he would have heard the roar. So he siphoned all the gas out of his snowmobile tank and got rid of it. Maybe he poured it into the tank on his pickup or maybe he just poured it away in the snow. Either way he stank up his garage with the gas fumes.

That was a new problem. He didn't want anyone coming along and smelling it. He locked the garage. It was the only way he knew to cover that. It was, of course, a stupid way. He locked the fumes in and he was dumb enough to think that in time they would dispel even though he was giving them nowhere to dispel to.

That brought him down to nothing but snowshoes. After everything had been quiet for a while out on the road, the snowshoes had been good enough to take him back to the car so he could put the empty dispatch case on the seat. This part of it was the way I'd been figuring it. He was so wrapped up in getting it back exactly where he had found it, that he didn't realize that when we'd pulled the body out of the car, it could only have been by sliding it across that seat.

That done, he had snowshoed over to Sobieski's place. He had to find the body so that he could put the keys in the old man's pocket. He could have put them in the car when he returned the case, but either they'd slipped his mind then and he didn't want to go back or else he thought it would be too many things for anyone to have overlooked while taking the body out of the car.

That would have been one of his reasons for going over to the Sobieskis. I would have been another. If he'd been watching from his house he could have been reasonably certain that it had been Stan snowmobiling out there and that Stan had taken the man he'd seen and that he hoped hadn't seen him over to his house.

While he was there, I went out. He had to wait till I was out of the way before he could go into the barn and put the keys in the old man's pocket. He watched me head back to the house and he went for the barn, but then I'd had the idea of stowing my skis away and turned back.

So he knocked me cold and dragged me off into the woods. I was supposed to lie there and freeze to death, but it didn't work. Stan came out to look for me and he came out before Dawson's trail had been wiped out by the wind and snow. Dawson's snowshoe tracks had been wiped out by his dragging me after him, and any tracks he'd left through the woods after leaving me had probably been covered over by the freshly fallen snow. They would have filled in quickly. The trail left by my body would have been deeper and would have taken longer to obliterate. It had led Stan to me.

In any case when Stan found me lying there, he would have looked no further. He would have been completely fixed on getting me up and back to the house as quickly as possible.

There had also been a third reason for Dawson to go to the Sobieski house. He had wanted to establish the fact that he was on snowshoes. Of all the people in the neighborhood who might be suspected, he was the one who would be in the clear. His snowmobile had been out of gas.

There was the locked house and the locked closet. Dawson

wasn't doing all this locking up because he was an old woman. He was a murderer and a thief. Behind that locked closet door or behind some other locked door in the place he had stowed the contents of the old man's dispatch case. He was taking no chances on anybody snooping around and coming on diamonds.

There was also his promise to Stan Sobieski, if Stan had ever exacted such a promise, and I doubted that. Stan had been keeping an eye on me but not that close an eye. Dawson had carried surveillance to farcical extremes. While I was outside, he had been reasonably loose in the way he had followed through on his so-called promise. Inside the house he had kept me under his eye through every moment. I'd tried the closet door, and he didn't want me wandering around trying any other locked doors.

Now I was even thinking of the plate of food he had carried upstairs for the King woman. He said she'd thrown it in his face, but it had been hot food and he'd come down with no scald marks on him. She said nobody had brought her anything. She was a liar, of course, but on this we should have believed her. He had never opened that bedroom door. He'd broken the plate and made a mess. He had been up there a long time, pretending that it had taken him that long to do a thorough cleanup, but he'd been using that time for exploring for the place where the dispatch case had been locked away. The dispatch case had been worrying him. Maybe he had been thinking fingerprints. Maybe he had wanted to find it and give it a rub-up.

I headed for the bedroom to get into my clothes and he was right there with me. Even now, when he'd told me how I could take it on the lam and was even pressuring me to do it, he couldn't still have been carrying through on any promise to Stan. He was pretending to be doing just that. I wondered whether he would take it all the way and go to the john when I was ready to take off. The way he was playing it, I expected he would. He had to lie to his neighbor and buddy. He was holding it down to the smallest possible lie.

"Time for me to go and take that crap," he said, after he'd unlocked the front door and seen me out of the house.

"My skis are in the garage," I reminded him. "You'll have to get them for me."

He scowled and snapped his fingers.

"Come on," he said.

He wasn't leaving me alone to go back into the house, not even for a moment and not even then. We went to the garage together. He unlocked it, pocketed his keys, and turned back to the house.

"Take them," he said, "and get going."

He went into the house.

"And that, my friend," I was thinking, "is your last mistake."

I left the skis and I jumped for his snowmobile. No chance now that the cops would pick me up out in the snow. I was going to pick them up at their barracks.

I dragged it out the garage door. I had just jumped aboard it when he came running out and saw me.

"Hey," he yelled as he jumped for me.

I was tempted to stay there and wait for him. Hand to hand and all even, it would have been a pleasure and nobody could say I didn't owe him. I owed him for the old man and I owed him for myself. I was even thinking that I owed him for Stan Sobieski, a good guy he'd been putting through hell. It was tempting, but I made a quick decision. It wouldn't be smart.

If I took him, I'd have to sit on him. And keep sitting on him through all those busy signals I'd be getting while I was trying to get through to the police barracks and then waiting till they came out to get him. The other way would be easier and cleaner. I just blast over to the barracks and fill them in on the score. Meanwhile he's the one on the phone getting the busy signals. When they'd get out to his place to pick him up, the way things had been going, he'd still be trying to get through to them to tell them about the killer who stole his snowmobile.

I went off on the snowmobile before he got within reach of me. I pointed it for the road. I was almost halfway to it when I heard that old air-tearing whistle go past my ear. It had been a long time since I'd last heard it, all the way back to the war; but that sound, if you've heard it once, you'll know it forever. You can comfort yourself with the thought that the ones you hear are the ones that have missed you. When you get hit, the rifle slug gets to you first. It trails its sound behind it.

It's small comfort, though, because you know that today's rifles aren't the old single-shot muzzle loaders. When one shot has come your way, it's got brothers who'll be right along trying to do better.

I left the straight course I'd been setting and put the snowmobile into a wildly swinging zigzag. On the zigs I could see the house door out of the corner of my eye. Good old peripheral vision showed me Dawson in the driveway standing with the rifle butt tucked into his shoulder and his cheek snuggled against the stock.

He fired again and again, but nothing came as close as that first shot. Those snowmobiles move but nowhere near as fast as a rifle slug and the zigzagging cut down on my forward progress. It was messing up his aim, but it was keeping me in range a longer time than I would have liked. Just before I hit the road, the ground took a dip that did it for me. I zoomed down into the hollow and took myself out of his sights.

If I headed cross-country, I wouldn't know the way and I was taking no chances on getting lost. I had to take the road and I knew that along where I'd be passing the old man's car I'd be riding high ground and he'd see me go by. But while it wasn't far enough to be out of rifle range—rifle range is a helluva long distance—it was far enough so that nobody could deal with it unless he was an expert marksman and then he'd have to have a telescopic sight.

I wasn't letting it bother me, but only when I was past that hump of snow that was the old man's car and the ground dipped down again, did I begin to relax.

Finding the turnoff was a breeze. I'd been over it with Stan, but with the snow, I wasn't certain that I'd recognize it. What I hadn't expected was that I would come on a clear track that would lead me right into it. There had been heavy snowmobile traffic that morning into the town and out, and no fresh snow had fallen over their tracks and there was no wind to drift them over.

I made the turning into the road to town, and I was almost down to the gas station when it hit me, and that was the one I didn't hear whistle past. It ripped a path across the sleeve of the sheepskin coat, but the damage to my arm was minimal. It came nowhere near the bone.

Even so, the glancing impact from a rifle slug will knock you off your feet. It knocked me off the snowmobile.

So there was Erridge, down and dazed and nothing to do but wait for the shot that was going to finish him. He wasn't so dazed that he wasn't doing some wondering, though. It could be that Dawson had been lucky and had slipped in between busy signals. The cops had come out, but what kind of cops go manhunting with rifles and come out shooting?

I tried to think Dawson. Back at the house he had been mighty quick with the rifle. He'd had it right handy and ready loaded. Obiously it had been part of his plan. Erridge, the fleeing murderer, was getting away on his skis, and he had to stop him. He had aimed to bring him down, but, so sorry, his shot had gone home and Erridge had gone down dead. Firing in a hurry at a moving target, even a great shot is likely to miss. It's just luck whether he misses his man entirely or misses the other way. Instead of just winging the fugitive, he's killed him.

It could have been so neat and now it was going to be, but how did Dawson get here all the way from the house? I'd left him down to nothing but the snowshoes and the rifle. Even if he'd taken a short cut, no man can be that speedy on snowshoes. There was no way I could work it out.

Then I heard it and it was coming at me. It wasn't another rifle shot, it was a snowmobile and it was coming down on me. I couldn't work that out either. I tried the thought of two snowmobiles—could he have had a second one stashed away somewhere? But two snowmobiles would have wrecked his cover. Nobody would believe both of them ran out of gas just as he got to his doorstep. No one could believe even one—two would be crazy.

It takes longer to tell about all this confused thinking than it took for me to tangle myself in my thoughts. These conflicting ideas weren't coming at me one by one in a neat parade of reasoning. They all came together in collision and contradiction.

The snowmobile stopped alongside me. I was trying to get to my feet and I wasn't making it. Landing in the deep snow,

I'd been spreadeagled and had therefore stayed pretty much on top of it. Let's say I was only half buried in it. Pulling my arms and legs together in the effort to get up out of it, I was consolidating my weight and that had me exerting heavier pressure on the soft snow. So instead of getting myself to my feet, I was just burying myself deeper in the snow.

With my face down in it, I couldn't see. I felt a hand take hold of my arm and then immediately let go and pull away. Before I could even begin to figure that, the hand was back and grabbing me by the other arm. With its help I made it to my feet. I was trying to blink the caked snow off my eyelashes. I couldn't see a thing. I was wearing what amounted to a snow blindfold.

Before I had my eyes cleared, he spoke. I knew the voice. It wasn't Dawson. It was Stan Sobieski. I was so busy adjusting to that shift, that it took me a moment before I could take in what he was saying.

"I wanted to think it wasn't you," he said.

I dug my hand into the pocket of my sheepskin. I wanted a handkerchief. Blinking wasn't doing much for me. I had to wipe the snow away from my eyes. I found something in my pocket but it wasn't a handkerchief. I left it. Whatever it was, it wasn't going to be any good for wiping my eyes clear.

"Who did you think you were shooting at?" I asked while I fumbled for the handkerchief in the other pocket of my coat.

"Oh, that," he said. "I knew it was you. I mean killing the old man."

I got the snow wiped away and I looked at him. If he had that haggard look of misery again, he also looked implacable.

"That what Dawson told you?" I asked.

He ignored my question. He had one of his own.

"Your arm?" he said. "Is it bad? You've been moving it and it doesn't seem to be bleeding much."

Looking down at it, I saw the rip in the sheepskin and a little blood.

"It's nothing," I said.

"I had to stop you."

"Before I got to the police?"

"That wasn't where you were going. Bert told me."

"I know what he told you. He told you I was going to the airport. He told you I was heading out. You know where the airport is. Was I headed that way?"

"You were headed to where you thought it was. He told me how you heard on the TV that it was open and they were flying. He told me that you asked all kinds of questions about where the airport was and he couldn't see why you needed to know, so he told you wrong. He told you this way."

"Just generally this way or did he give you the details he gave me?"

"He was stuck. You'd taken his snowmobile. He got me on the phone and told me you got away from him. He had to tell me just which way you were going so I could come cross-country and catch up with you."

"He told me to come into this road and take the first left turning," I said. "He told me that was the airport road. So I'm here. I didn't take that turning. I stayed with this road because I knew what was down here—the gas station and the dairy and then the police barracks. When she was worrying about your being so long, Sally told me where the police barracks was. She said only a little way beyond the dairy, between the dairy and the town."

"You expect me to believe you swiped his snowmobile so you could go to the barracks and turn yourself in?"

"I expect you to believe I stole his snowmobile so I could get to the police and turn Dawson in. I bet he told you that I was dangerous. I bet he told you that as soon as you caught up with me, you were to take no chances. He told you to shoot to kill. Is that where he slipped, thinking you were such a great rifle shot that you couldn't miss?"

"Yeah, he told me, but I didn't have to do that. Winging you was enough. Bert Dawson's an old woman. Look at the way he keeps everything locked up."

"That's right," I said. "Look at that. Look at what he's got locked away because he's afraid someone might find it and know he killed the old man and robbed him."

I was pulling off my glove and going back down into that pocket where I'd felt something. Sobieski backed away a little and brought his rifle to bear on me.

"Don't go for a gun," he said.

It didn't sound like an order. It sounded as though he was pleading with me. He was asking me not to make him take another shot at me.

"No gun," I said. "There's something in my pocket. I felt it through my gloves. I don't know what it is, but it shouldn't be there. It wasn't there when I left your place with Dawson. Somebody put it there and there was nobody but Dawson."

"All right," he said. "Bring it out."

He was ready with his rifle. He could take the chance. I couldn't be such a quick draw that he wouldn't be quicker with the rifle. After all, he didn't have to draw at all. He already had it on target.

It was a small brown flannel bag tied closed with a drawstring. It felt as though it had a few small pebbles in it. I opened it and turned three small diamonds out into my palm.

In that light—sun, and snowglare—they were dazzling. I looked at them and I looked at Sobieski. He winced.

"You kill a man for that?" he said.

"Not me," I said, "and not for these. He did it for a lot more. These were what he had to sacrifice to pin it on me while he goes scot free with the rest."

Sobieski was troubled.

"You say him and he says you," he mumbled.

I ran it down for him: the snowmobile that saw me and went away, the key, the dispatch case, the conveniently empty snowmobile tank, the gas stench in the garage that had to be from a siphoning job, the attack on me, the locked house, the locked garage, the locked closet, the diamonds that hadn't been on me when I left to go home with Dawson and that were on me now.

"You went through all my pockets," I reminded him. "You don't have to take my word for it that they weren't on me then. You know."

"If you had them in your car," Stan said, "you wouldn't be leaving them there and take off without them. On your way over here you stopped by your car and picked them up."

"You came cross-country," I told him. "I came by the road. I saw my car and you didn't. At least I saw the hump of snow that has Baby under it. I'd have to dig down to get at it. Did I have the time for that? You don't have to bother to figure the time. You can just go and look at my car. You'll see the way it's buried, a smooth mound of snow untouched since it last fell and not a flake's been falling this morning since I pulled away from Dawson's place."

He believed me. He'd been wanting to believe.

"Let's go on to the barracks," he said. "They've got to know about Bert. I never much liked the son of a bitch, but I'd never have thought."

That was the way it went. He'd liked Erridge from the first, but from the first he had thought. I couldn't hold that against him since it went both ways. I'd liked him from the first and from the first I'd also been thinking.

We blasted on down to the police barracks and told our story. Then it was on into the town to the hospital for a dressing on my arm. He stayed with me all the way. Coming out of the hospital, he still had one thing bothering him.

"There's a hotel here in town," he said, "and a couple of decent motels till the road's open and you can roll again, though maybe you shouldn't for a while with your arm."

They'd bandaged me up and put the arm in a sling, but Baby and I are a team. I can handle her one-handed.

"I'll be okay," I said.

"Sure you will. I'm thinking of me. As soon as Sally hears I took that shot at you and creased your arm, I'm going to be in trouble with her again. The trouble won't be as bad if I bring you home with me. You know Sally. She'll feel better about it if she gets to fuss over you."

"I know Sally," I said. "I'm going to like having her fuss over me."

He broke out the grin and was about to clap me on the back, but he remembered and he put his hand away without doing it. After all, Erridge was walking wounded.